HORSEMEN
FROM HELL

HORSEMEN FROM HELL

HOMER HATTEN

CUTTING EDGE

ISBN-13: 978-1-954840-87-4

Published by
Cutting Edge Books
PO Box 8212
Calabasas, CA 91372
www.cuttingedgebooks.com

HORSEMEN FROM HELL

CHAPTER ONE

ITCHFIELD LANDING, ARKANSAS, was a muddy point of treeless land, jutting out into the Mississippi just where the White River emptied into it, a darkly hostile barrier of sodden and rain-soaked timber rising behind it, and a dark, late-afternoon sky above it. There was an unpainted, rain-rotten wharf that sagged in misery and decay when the river packet *Dixie Rose* thrust the shore end of its gangplank to it.

There were only two buildings upon the spit of land. The nearer, larger one, sag-roofed above its walls of peeling logs, had a rough stone chimney at either end. The narrow door was standing ajar and the scant, square windows were battened shut with solid shutters. The other log building was miserly and square and unwindowed, with a single door.

Staring incredulously around her, Melissa McCutcheon had thought at first that it was a stable, until she saw the lank woman and the knot of unwashed, ragged brats come out of it and knew that it was their home.

A dismal drizzle of rain shadowed the water and the land and the two wretched cabins and the slack-jawed woman and her brood. It brought the sour smell of rotting wood and decayed vegetation up from the swamp behind the wall of trees, and almost smothered the deep roar of the *Dixie Rose's* triple-toned whistle and the mechanical, fitful cursing of the bucko mate who leaned from the rail of the. Texas deck to swear at the Negroes running out the plank.

She had come out of the captain's cabin with the five hundred dollars her brother-in-law had promised her in crisp new Dixie bills folded inside a handkerchief and tucked away in the depths of her reticule. The captain had been impatient, a little relieved to be rid of her.

"You'll be catching a White River steamer from here up to Springfield, then?" he'd said brusquely.

"Yes," Melissa said. "Yes, of course. I'm going to join my husband in Springfield. He went out from Kentucky several months ago and now I'm—I'm going to him."

The captain nodded, but his face told her plainly enough what he thought of a man who'd let his wife make such a trip alone. "Well," he said gruffly, "I hope you won't have to wait too long for that packet. These White River boats don't pretend to keep a schedule. Might be one along tomorrow and there might not be one for a month. And such accommodations as you'll find here at Litchfield while you're waiting aren't what you'd call luxurious."

"They'll serve," she said shortly. She'd caught the look in his face, a reflection of a look she'd seen on too many faces since Jeff ran away and left her, and she wanted no more of it. She thanked him with a chill rigidity in her voice and turned to the gangplank.

The young purser had gone to the gangplank with her and ordered two of the Negroes to carry her brassbound trunk ashore, where they had deposited it in the inch-deep slime of mud that covered the sagging dock. Two more Negroes took her carpetbags ashore and piled them on top of the trunk. The purser himself had taken her arm to help her down the swaying gangplank and lifted his hat and pointed out the larger building with the solid plank shutters.

"That's Merigay's Tavern, if you can call it a tavern," he'd said. It's the best there is, and it's all there is here, I'm afraid."

"Merigay's Tavern!" she'd echoed in a sort of dazed disbelief. The purser glanced at her and started to speak again and then apparently thought better of it. He simply lifted his hat for the second time and turned back to the gangplank and to the confident order and the linen tablecloths and the sense of civilization that was the *Dixie Rose.*

The slattern woman and the litter of lank-haired, filthy children around her stared suspiciously at Melissa across the twenty feet of muddy earth that separated them. Melissa began to walk across the slippery wharf toward them, seeing two of the smaller children run and hide their faces behind their mother's skirts.

"Are you Mrs. Merigay? Are you the woman who owns that—that tavern over there?"

The woman's eyes widened in momentary alarm and then seemed to sink deeper into her head, back into wary taciturnity.

"Ain't no Mrs. Merigay. Not since Aunt Corrie went on to the saints. Jobe had him a flibberty-gibbet from somewheres out in the swamp, but they wasn't never wed an' she lit a shuck with a trapper."

Merciful God! Melissa thought hopelessly. She turned her head a little, pretending to survey the tavern while she fought her way back out of a horror of disbelief and into the hard-held appearance of a cool adequacy that she certainly did not feel. "Who looks after the tavern, then? Travelers stay there, don't they? And there is some provision for them to eat and sleep while they're here?"

"Ain't many travelers come this way. Keelboaters stay aboard, an' the swampers ain't never here unless they got hides to trade for liquor an' gunpowder. An' when they come—Lawd! They don't want nothin' but swillin' an' fightin' and pushin' up to Jobe's gal-child, if she ain't already took to th' timber."

It was like trying to carry on a conversation with someone who had no inkling of her language or her needs. She had a swift, ridiculous vision of herself standing there in the soft ooze of the mud with the rain beating down on her through unending days and nights while she flung her hopeless questions against the baffling digressions of this sluttish female.

Melissa turned and went back to the wharf for her luggage, trying to hold her head up and walk briskly and surely, but finding the rain and the wind pushing at her until she bowed her head to meet them while the soft mud trapped her and turned her quick step into a pace that was not much better than a shuffle.

The tavern was on a slightly rising knoll of barren ground, and she had to lean forward and push herself into the wind to make headway against the little slope. Behind her, by the joined rivers, the woman and the staring, ragged children watched her without a sound, their faces almost incurious, only their heads turning slowly, like joined balls upon identical pivots, as she went past them and up the slope and in through the sagging doorway of the tavern.

The stink of it assailed her in the instant that she stepped inside. The door that she had used, as far as she could see, was the only opening through which fresh air could penetrate the place. A gray, cobwebbed darkness was everywhere, shadowing the cold stone hearth directly across from her, the two doorways on either side that led into adjacent rooms, the uneven floor of hard-packed earth, the table and the four stools and the half-cured deer and coon and 'possum hides pegged against the clay-chinked log walls. The room was no more than twelve feet square, its sagging ceiling pierced by a hole in one corner that was reached by a rough ladder of unpeeled poles spiked into the wall.

Melissa called out but no one answered, and then she saw the tallow dip on the table, its wick supported above the dish by a twisted loop of wire that ran down to the dish's edge. There was flint and steel beside it, and she stripped off her fine kid gloves, and put the carpetbag and the reticule down, brushing away a clot of food to make a place for them. But the steel slipped in her fingers when she took it up, and the flint was worn smooth along one edge. She centered them above the wick again and struck downward viciously, seeing the thin chain of sparks fly out and down and into the wick, and she bent forward to breathe on it until a little rim of red appeared, and then a thin finger of flame, and finally a rough blaze that cast an uncertain circle of light across the table and, faintly, into the corners of the room.

There was a pile of wood and kindling beside the black-mawed hearth, and Melissa had begun to lay a fire in it to drive out the chill of the rain and the March wind when she heard a man cough from the room off to the right. Then she heard the sound of heavy boots scuffling across the dirt floor toward the room where she was.

She jerked up her head, wide-eyed in sudden alarm, and some instinct made her pick up the tallow dip and replace it on the puncheon table and then move quickly and silently so that the weight and breadth of the table were between her and the door that opened into the other room. She made herself stand erect, the way her Grandmother Rhea had taught her that a woman of pride and good family should stand—not leaning against the table or resting her fingertips against it, but away from it and sure of herself. One hand was folded lightly and held in the palm of the other, and the wide black eyes were intent and faintly luminous. The tip of her tongue moistened the rich lower lip that was a little too wide and too full for real beauty, and yet held a promise that all men saw and understood.

The man came through the door then, and she caught her breath and felt her throat suddenly tight and swollen and threw a sharp, quick glance at the outer doorway without consciously thinking of it as a way of escape. In the slivered instant that she looked at it and then back at him, she knew that it was too far away and that he was already between her and any sanctuary it might have offered.

She had never seen a man like this before, not even on the brawling river rafts that she'd sometimes watched going down the Ohio, or in the savage canebrake settlements where Jeff had taken her on two of his hunting trips. He was naked above the waist, a nakedness hidden and yet made more unmistakable by the tangled mat of hair that covered his chest, belly, arms, and shoulders. He had the face of a devil, unshaven, his hair a wild tumult of spiky points and his eyes red-rimmed. The grease-stained, filthy trousers that hung loosely from his hips were ripped and torn, their tattered legs tucked into boots slimy with the mud of the swamp.

He steadied himself with one hand against the doorframe, swaying a little, and she caught the stench of cheap liquor and stale sweat upon him even across the room. The clawed fingers of one hand scraped at his ribs. Abruptly, he belched gustily, swaying and catching himself again and she jerked her head away from the sight of him and felt the black iciness of fear gathering below her heart.

"You been God's own long time gittin' here!"

His voice was contemptuously abusive, the growling truculence of a man too long deprived of his just deserts.

"Two months ago I give your Uncle Braden that pile of hides. Two months ago he give me his solemn oath he'd send you up here to me by the first packet that come up the river."

Without turning he spat on the dirt floor halfway between them.

"I don't know what you're talking about!" Melissa cried.

The sharp gusts of her breath were panting waves pounding against the laboring headlands of her breasts.

"I'm Melissa Rhea—" Why did I suddenly, and without thinking of it, give this man my maiden name instead of the name I had from Jeff McCutcheon, she thought with a quick gasp of wonder. "I came in on the *Dixie Rose*. I want to find a boat to take me up the White River to Springfield. I don't have any Uncle Braden! And nobody sent me here to you!"

"Damn you, don't you lie to me!" His eyes tightened into bloodshot slits of anger and the unshaven upper lip twisted back into a snarl of yellow teeth and gray-blue lips.

"I can tell from them fancy riggin's, you got on you been sportin' up an' down the river with every Tom, Dick an' Harry that'd have you, instead of makin' your way here direct, like Braden told you. But you an' him ain't goin' to skin me outa them hides. I ain't goin' to be whipsawed by no swaller-tailed slut that figures she's too fancy for ol' Jobe Merigay!"

"But it's not like that, I tell you! I'll get out of here—"

"You ain't goin' nowhere!" He lunged toward her with one massive paw sweeping up in the beginning of a blow. "I'll learn ye your lesson now!"

She tried to scream and to turn and run from him, but she was paralyzed with terror. Her mouth jerked in a wild, soundless shrieking and her hands flew up in a furious effort to fend him off. She fell back, her feet awkward as lumps of lead beneath the trembling numbness of her legs, beneath the awful, down-pulling fear that was in her.

"But you're wrong! You don't understand! Nobody sent me—you've got to wait! Please—please let me tell you—"

The words turned into a blind and senseless screaming, escaping in a frantic wail of terror, a wrenching and a ripping free of horror that clamored, panic-stricken, in the smoky room. The great hand cuffed at her and she threw up her arm to guard against the blow, feeling it suddenly agonized and battered as the fierce sledge of his fist knocked it aside. The hand drove on as if the fending arm had been no more than a breath of air, tearing at the collar of her dress, ripping it down and away, jerking her forward in the instant before the cloth gave way, taking the rose colored camisole and the whalebone-stayed corselet with it, so that suddenly, incredibly and horribly, she was naked from chin to waist, exposed as no man except Jeff had ever seen her.

"Oh, Mother of God! Oh—merciful Mary—"

She clawed at him with hands that opened red gashes down his face, thrusting at his eyes, trying to keep the table between them but seeing it wrenched aside as he leaned across it, striking at her and clawing at her and jerking her toward him.

"You beast! You animal! You—"

He jerked at her naked arm, swinging her around like a puppet on a string, and as she whirled her outstretched hand struck the tallow dip that had fallen over on its side and now flared in a widening circle of stinking grease and sharply bubbling fire. Her fingers closed on the greasy dish, feeling the fire lick at her and not caring. She brought it up as a man would swing a scythe, forcing it toward his face. It became a part of him, the fire and the flaming, searing oil, clinging and fastening upon his beard.

He threw up his hands, beating at his face, howling in a wildly furious outpouring of terrorized horror. Gasping, screaming, he fell back with his mouth open and twisted and shocked, unbelieving sound pouring from it. The grease dripped down from his chin, blazing red-yellow, and lodged in the matted hair upon his chest.

The man tried to turn and run toward the open door, toward the wet dusk and the drizzling rain. His foot struck one of the three-legged stools that crouched like dogs against the floor. As his arms shot out to save himself, his whole body plunged forward, falling in a wild confusion of threshing arms and legs and torch-lit body. The hoarse screaming seemed not to come out of his throat, but to be the anguish forced out of the bones and flesh of his body.

She heard herself screaming as he went down, her body still leaning tensely across the tilted table as it had been when she thrust the fire upon him, her eyes wide with terror. Her clothing hung in tatters around her waist so that the revealed bare column of her body with its naked, rose-pointed breasts rose like a dimly seen statue in a murky room, a statue still inviolate, but stained by the tide of violence and insult that had broken about it. She screamed again, her head thrown back and her clenched fists grinding into her lips, her eyes locked upon the writhing body that agonized upon the floor.

Melissa realized suddenly that there was another woman's voice, screaming against her own, and she jerked around to see a swirling of red calico skirts already halfway down the pole ladder from the loft and catch a glimpse of a woman's twisted face—a girl's face?—spitting hatred at her as she ran into the adjoining room and ran back again with a dirty, rough-quilted bed covering in her hands. She threw it over the man and threw herself down with it and smothered out the flames, and then threw the quilt aside and turned, on her knees, to glare up at Melissa.

Melissa became abruptly aware of her nakedness and began to pull the tatters of her clothing around her with fingers that trembled. The girl was screaming at her, and the man was groaning and twisting, but more than half unconscious now, with his face down against the floor and the slow smoke still rising softly from his body.

"You're a woman, ain't you?" the girl shouted. "You ain't made to treat a man that way!"

The furious anger, the sudden, incredible sense of the idiocy and the futility of the scene they were playing swept the fear out of Melissa to leave her acidly contemptuous and rapier hard. "If you think it's all right to do what he wanted me to—you do it! But I'm getting out of here. I'm getting out right now." She snatched up her things, drawing the cloak about her.

"Sometimes I wish I could, when he's took so, an' him a lone widow man. But he's my pappy."

"You mean that man is your father?"

"I'm Pansy Merigay."

This, then, was the girl the slattern woman had mentioned. The girl that the swampers, the drunken trappers would be "pushing up to" when they came in to Merigay's Tavern. Melissa forced herself to look at her, to see her plainly without the fog of fear and anger and violence shuddering uneasily between them.

A yellow-haired girl, the hair brittle brown now and caked with dirt. She had blue eyes, as blue as the pansies that had given her their name, and a sharp-pointed, gamin face above the ragged calico that obviously had nothing beneath it except the still not matured body.

"Then you can't leave him like that."

It was no instinct of pity or of attempted requital for the injuries she had inflicted upon Merigay that had brought the words to her lips. Melissa continued, "He's not dead—and I don't think he's going to die. You have some salve, and an old bed sheet? Get whatever you've got and I'll help you with him. After that we'll decide what else has to be done."

"We ain't needin' no help from such as you—" But the girl's voice was uncertain. "Well—seems like I ought—"

Abruptly, the girl turned and ran into the room opposite the one from which the man had lurched. Her voice came back, still shrill, still threatening. "You do him a damage, I swear I'll cut your heart out."

Melissa put the reticule and the carpetbag down on the table again, tugging the table erect and feeling the grease from the tallow dip slippery and still hot against her fingers. She folded the cloak and put it aside, knowing her own half-nakednes did not matter here.

She took the man's arm and pulled it up and backward, throwing her weight against his, ignoring the sharp sounds of pain that came from his lips and the weakened resistance he tried to offer.

"Turn over, damn you," she said sharply, pressing the words out between her teeth. "Turn over where we can get at you."

He screamed, once, as his body shifted and then he was on his back and his burnt mouth was gaping open and the eyes were blank, staring at the smoke-stained ceiling. The girl came back into the room, running, with a crumpled fold of cloth and a yellow earthen crock in her hands. Her eyes were still fiercely angry and her voice was bitter as she slammed the crock down on the table and faced Melissa for an instant before she scooped up a handful of the grease and turned back to the burned man on the floor.

"You're ridin' high an' mighty now." The words were as venomous as poisoned arrows. "But tomorrow night's when Burr Keltin an' his swampers come to the landing. He's a mean man, Burr Keltin is; you'll change when he lays his hands on you!"

CHAPTER TWO

I<small>T WAS PAST DARK</small> of the second day, and she had bribed Pansy Merigay to hide her in the tavern attic until Keltin and his swampers had come and caroused and gone. She'd tried it first with the offer of two crisp Dixie notes, but that hadn't been enough to bury the girl's fear of Burr Keltin under her hungry covetousness. It was then that Melissa had offered her a gold-fili-greed vial of perfume. The blue eyes had widened and the mouth had tightened and sharpened a little as the girl reached out her work-roughened hand for it.

The bargain had been struck. She was to supply Melissa with a loaded pistol and hide her in the attic while Keltin was at the landing. She was to say nothing to anyone about Melissa's presence at Litchfield Landing. And she was to keep Keltin and his men out of the attic at all costs.

Hidden there, lying very still on the pallet Pansy had made for her, exhausted and yet as fine-drawn as a rapier blade, she could look up through the cracks and the warped and twisted wind vanes in the roof and see the sleety storm that shut out the windy night sky and battered like incessant hammers against the shake shingles. But it was better and safer to watch below, to be on guard.

She had identified Keltin at once. There'd been no mistaking him from the instant the bows of the swampers' scooped-out log dugouts grated into the river bank at dusk and the boisterous invasion began. Keltin was a big man, gross-bodied as a bull. She'd had an impression of a fiery thatch of coarse hair that was like a Norseman's cap, and a tangle of red beard and a heavy body that was thick-barreled and virile. His voice had boomed and roared at the fierce-eyed horde of men behind him. She'd turned cold watching him, feeling her spirit and her courage collapse into horror at the thought of falling into his hands.

And the men with him were no better; there was evil in all of them.

They had been there for an hour now—long enough for them all to be more than half drunk and for the girl, Pansy, to have been mauled and mishandled, with her dress half ripped off and her hair disheveled and her face red with excitement and whisky.

Melissa twisted her head away from the yellow cracks of light beside the pallet. There was a nightmare incredulity that she should be here, trapped beneath the same roof that held those brutal people. She could feel her whole body trembling. She turned her head so that she looked out through the long, empty slot where the slanted roof eaves lifted half a dozen inches from the wall of peeling logs.

It was then that she first saw Mallonee and the Cherokees, when they rode out of the river-bank darkness and into the gray paleness of the sleet-beaten oval of Litchfield Landing.

At first they were only shapeless, hooded, bent-backed figures, their heads and backs bent against the storm. They rode in toward the cabin and a shaft of light from a sagging window shutter caught them. She saw that the man who rode in the lead was a white man, and that the others were turbaned Indians in long, tight-belted, tanned-hide hunting coats. The light caught their brown, ominous faces.

They pulled the lean, ice-maned horses to a stop a dozen feet from the door, and the white man and the Indian who rode at his flank turned in their saddles and talked together, inaudible beneath the howling wind. The Indian was doubtful and wary, the white man coldly angry and impatient. She felt another pulse of terror run through her at the sight of them. The men in the room below were brawlers, ruffians; but the men outside were the wolf pack, the killers, cold-eyed men of blood and death.

The leader brought one hand down peremptorily, like a man slashing away argument and disagreement with the edge of a brutal blade. The Indian stared at him without moving, and yet she knew that the white man's decision had been irrevocable. They turned then, the long line of them, and rode into the lean-to that served as a stable. Melissa knew that they too were to become a part of the brawling tumult inside the tavern.

She whirled, raising her body off the pallet, to stare down through the wide cracks as the tumult in the room below erupted in a sudden explosion of shattering violence. A table slammed and cracked against the wall. A voice snarled in rising fury, and a man's body crashed hard against the floor. Two of the swampers—one young, yellow-haired and wolf-eyed, the other an older, heavier, black-bearded man—were on the floor. Fists and teeth and boots clawed and slashed and hammered against each other, ripping and shredding clothing and flesh away. Their angry snarls filled the room, coming up to her in an unending roar of tooth-and-claw savagery.

Their companions pressed around them, urging them on. Only Keltin was withdrawn from the berserk fury. At the side of the fireplace, one elbow resting on the axe-hewed mantle and the other arm hard around wide-eyed, screaming Pansy, he watched the fight with the half-contemptuous, half-derisive look of a warrior watching two children squabble and scream in a village street.

She saw the white man and four of the Indians come out of the shanty stable, the sleet frozen on them, their bodies bulky but quick moving as they rounded the end of the tavern and struck open the front door. The swampers whirled to stare at them, and Keltin jerked up his head and glared as he pushed himself away from the fireplace.

On the floor, the yellow-headed boy and the black-bearded man bellowed and bawled and swore, tearing and gouging, so wrapped in their own violence that these strangers did not exist for them. The bedraggled girl's mouth was frozen half opened.

Keltin's body seemed to harden and tense itself. "We need no strangers here tonight. Get out! Get out of here!" He moved out into the room, fists clenched, head dropped between his shoulders.

"Stand back, man. Watch them, my brothers," the white man cautioned.

The stranger had a voice like a deep-toned bar of tempered steel, Melissa thought. He wore the same scarlet figured, tight-wrapped turban as his Indians, the same hunting coat with the naked knife thrust through the front knot of the belt. And he was as tautly ominous as a tiger. He was a tall man in his early thirties, black-browed and black-haired, with a swordsman's hips and a wrestler's shoulders—and a gentleman, there was no mistaking that. Keltin was no more than a red-faced brawler, a dung-heap rooster ruffling against a falcon.

And Burr Keltin knew it. With an almost personal sense of satisfaction, Melissa saw him hesitate, saw the glare die a little in his eyes, his truculence fading.

"You hunt for trouble, you'll find it here."

But there was a doubt in the red-bearded blusterer's voice now. Unadmitted, there was a cringing willingness to come to terms.

"We're not hunting trouble." The white man's contempt was an insult. "I'm Mallonee—Dale Mallonee, from Colquitt County, Mississippi. We're traveling north, and we'll stay here tonight."

"Not them Indians. Not while I'm here."

It was hard for Keltin to abandon his role of tyrant with the eyes of his men upon him.

"They're Cherokees. My mother was half Cherokee. Where I go, they go. And there'll be two more here as soon as they've unsaddled our horses."

It was a flat statement, Melissa realized, not a basis for discussion, not even a challenge; for he wouldn't dignify Keltin as an equal or worth-while adversary. But his eyes were glowing, as if red coals of pent-up violence and impatience were piled up behind them. They jerked down as the two whirling combatants on the floor spun and crashed against his knees.

"By hell, now!" he said huskily. "By all the saints—"

The violence and impatience Melissa had seen bottled in him exploded now in a murderous outburst that drove his boot deep into the belly of the sandy-haired brawler, ripping shirt and flesh away as the suddenly limp body slammed back into the center of the room. The black-bearded man was immediately upon it; his knife rose and fell swiftly and blood spurted from the younger man's throat. He gasped, and drew up his knee and beat his hands against the floor in agony. Then the knees slowly slackened and the body finally lay quite still.

The black-bearded man looked up, crouching still, his eyes red-rimmed, a yellow slaver of spittle draining from the corner of his mouth.

"I told him I'd kill him did he keep pushin' me," he said hoarsely. His eyes went around the circle of faces like the eyes of a wild animal searching the bars of a cage. "I said I'd do it an' I done it!"

The white man, Mallonee, was staring at him with disgusted anger hardening his face. For an instant Melissa had the impression that he despised himself for having been drawn into such butchery. Then it was gone, and he was looking across the room at Keltin again.

"One of your men?" he said, and his voice was icy.

"No more'n th' others." Anger fought against the reluctant wariness in the red-haired man, flushing his face, deepening his voice into a sound like grating stones. He whirled to stare at the black-bearded man, who had lifted himself to his feet and was swaying a little, still wrapped in the red maze of fury and killing.

"Damn your slimy guts!" Keltin's rage was lusty. "You've killed a man worth more to me than a dozen whelps such as you! An' now you can't do no more than stand there an' gawk at him." The bull voice boomed up in a sudden explosion of sound that seemed to rock the room. "If you can't do nothin' else, get him out from underfoot! Get him outa my sight!"

The big man turned and stooped, clawing at the dead man's arms and shoulders, dragging and rolling and shoving him across the floor and past Mallonee and the Indians and out the door. In the silence that followed, Pansy slipped away from the corner of the fireplace and came sidling across the room until she was directly in front of Mallonee. She smirked up at him.

"We'll be plumb proud to have you join us—" She caught the icy rebuff of his stare and changed the phrase with a servile quickness—"or stay any way you're a mind to. There's stew cooked in the kitchen, an' you can bed down there—"

"We'll take a look at it. You've got whisky out there, too?"

"You'll find a keg of corn squeezin's handy, an' there's cups an' platters a-plenty."

He jerked his head, and the four Cherokees followed him as he turned away toward the kitchen doorway, heedless of the swampers who fell back silent now and gaping as he shouldered through them.

In the bare, wind-swept attic above him Melissa caught her breath, her fingers twisting and tightening the blankets of the pallet. Keltin had been a danger, a danger that was like a plunging avalanche, furious and unpredictable—but blind, and therefore capable of being tricked and confused and eluded. But this other man was an unknown factor, as vital and as inescapable as a lance of lightning.

The outside door of the central room slammed open and shut. The black-bearded man had come in again, and the slattern woman Melissa had seen with her first glimpse of Litchfield Landing was with him. The swampers gathered around her, and she turned from one to the other and laughing shrilly.

"Law' me!" She threw up her bony hands in pretended confusion. "I can't take care of this many fine, strappin' men! Pansy, you goin' to help me, or are they goin' to git a whack at that fancy one come in so high an' mighty off th' steam packet yesterday?"

Melissa's heart froze inside her. She saw Pansy shoot a quick glance up to the trap door that led into the attic and then bite her lip and shake her head at the older woman in a sign that enjoined secrecy. But the damage was done. The swampers were crowding around the woman, their voices excited and demanding. Burr Keltin forced his way through them, his heavy arms brushing them aside till he was face to face with the vixen in the torn, unwashed dress.

"Who's this you're talkin' about? You got someone here at th' landin' I ain't set eyes on?"

The woman seemed to quail away from him as if his nearness planted sudden fear in her. Her eyes shot across the room to Pansy and she wet her lips with her tongue as she tried to stammer out an answer.

"Why—why, I don't know nothin' about her. I swear to God, Burr, I don't! She come flouncin' in here yesterday off th' *Dixie Rose,* all primped up in silks an' satins an' wearin' diamonds bigger'n apples on her fingers. But she come straight in here an' she ain't been out since, far as I know. I reckon maybe Pansy can tell you about her, though, if she's a mind to."

Keltin swung back around to Pansy, and Melissa saw the girl shrink back against the wall as his head came down and his eyes bored into hers.

"All right," he growled. "Let's hear ye speak your piece damn fast."

"I was—I was just fixin' to tell you, Burr." The girl's hands writhed together. Fear had drained the blood out of her cheeks. "She named herself Melissa Rhea at first, but then later she let me know her last name was McCutcheon. She's come outa Kentucky bound for some place up in Missouri. She's hidin' up yonder in th' loft, if you're minded to take a look at her—"

Mallonee and one of the Indians had come to the kitchen doorway and Melissa saw his face sharpen into startled inquiry at the sound of her name, for the McCutcheons of Kentucky were a legend in the South—a legend of endless acres and armies of slaves and fine horses and great mansions and wealth and privilege and power. Mallonee was a gentleman of Mississippi, and he would know of them.

The thought snapped like a broken thread as Burr Keltin jumped for the ladder leading up to the loft. She gathered her legs under her, scrambling up from the pallet in blind terror, feeling her fingers close around the butt of the single-shot pistol Pansy had given her.

Stumbling, gasping, she scrambled toward the most distant corner of the sag-roofed attic, wedging herself down in the narrow angle beneath the eaves in a frantic effort at concealment. The square of light that had been the trap-door opening was distorted, blotted out, as Keltin's head and shoulders came thrusting through it. And then he was in the attic with her, his heavy boots hammering on the rough planks of the floor, his head thrust forward, turning from side to side as he searched the patchwork pattern of light and darkness.

"Come out of there, wherever you're hid! Come out an' Burr Keltin'll learn ye some things about a man ye never knowed before."

He moved away from the light, turning toward the corner where she was hidden, and his voice exploded in a roar of animal triumph.

"I see you! Come out of it, now—"

He plunged forward and she pushed herself up and away from the wall, running and dodging frantically, twisting past the edge of his grasping fingertips. He turned and followed her. The pistol jerked up in her hand as she turned to face him, and she heard her own voice screaming in a hopeless, desperate defiance.

"Stand back! Stand back or I'll kill you! I'll shoot—I'll—"

The pistol jerked and barked in her hand, the sound of it distorted beneath the shallow roof. Keltin whooped in delight, rushing toward her, and she knew that she had missed him.

They were fighting like wildcats then, her screaming rising hysterically above the sound of his trampling boots and his drunken cursing. She felt his hands hard on her body, felt herself twisted and jerked and thrown off balance, felt his breath hot against her face. And suddenly, through the blind haze and horror of it, she heard Mallonee's voice crack and crackle in the room below.

"Watch out behind me!"

Keltin's fist drove into her face and as fire flared inside her brain and the pain was like a shower of knives she went down with his body crushing upon her. She clawed at him like a cat, her nails ripping at his eyes, raking the unshaven flesh from his heavy jowls. He jerked back and in the instant of release she was up and on her feet and trying to run, and he was on his feet again and after her, his heavy fist swinging at her as he ran. There was no place for her to go, and in an instant he had her again, his arms like heavy bars that she could not escape. He swung her around and in the shattering instant she saw that Mallonee was in the attic and was charging toward them. They were almost face to face, her back against Keltin's chest and his arm across her throat as he pulled her body into a quivering arc that choked her into helplessness.

The knife came out of Mallonee's belt as he drove in. Keltin saw him then and swung the woman around so that she was a shield between the knife and his own body. Mallonee went in high, with the knife driving by just an inch above her shoulder, trying for Keltin's throat and missing it by just enough for the blade to bury itself in the heavy shoulder muscles. Keltin yelled and she felt his body go backward as Mallonee freed the knife.

She went down at Mallonee's feet, her hands clutching at her throat. He cleared her in a leap and pushed the attack home, driving at Keltin's throat and chest with the knife, forcing him back until his shoulders were against the flat gable end of the loft.

The swamper's own knife was out by then, and he dodged to one side, moving with a hard, taut agility, to lunge out at Mallonee with a wicked uppercut that would have ripped him open from guts to chin if Mallonee had not twisted to one side as the knife flashed. Mallonee went in low then, slashing at his belly and drawing blood across his ribs before Keltin's knife came down in a backhand stroke that went into Mallonee's hunting shirt just at the shoulder and sliced it open down to the belt.

The knife hung there and in the instant that Mallonee was off balance, Keltin's left arm shot out and his hand closed around Mallonee's right wrist, twisting it until it cracked in an effort to shake the knife out of Mallonee's hand. It seemed to Mallonee that his whole arm had suddenly gone numb, and as he felt the hilt of the knife slipping out of his fingers he whirled enough to bring his left hand around and catch the knife with it.

But one hand was as good as the other as far as he was concerned. That was a knack the Indians had drilled into him when he was a boy, learning the tricks of knife-play on the bare wrestling ground of the Cherokee village that had squatted on his father's plantation. He cut at Keltin and caught him just enough to swing him away from the gable and back toward the center of the room and the gaping hole of the trap door. The swamper was breathing hard, but he was turning desperate, too. He'd have to be finished soon or not at all, Mallonee thought grimly.

The swamper went backward, holding Mallonee off with his knife lashing back and forth like a striking snake. Suddenly he jerked to one side and came at Mallonee with the knife down and his arm straight and stiff as if the arm and the knife had been a bayonet on the end of a rifle. The point grazed Mallonee's shoulder, in spite of his quick jerk to one side, and for an instant they faced each other, Keltin's arms down and his body still leaning forward a little, Mallonee's own knife ready just at the level of his belt.

He gathered himself like a cat and went up and forward in a single motion, the point of his knife driving in just below Keltin's chin.

Keltin shouted in agony as he went backward with his arms thrown out and his legs kicking at the floor. His shoulders crashed against the edge of the trap door hole in the floor, and he smashed through it, down into the midst of the swampers. They fell back, shouting and trampling on each other.

Mallonee went down through the trap door after him. The Cherokees hadn't waited for orders. By the time Mallonee had his feet under him, he could see their knives flashing as the swampers were pushed back into a corner with the yellow stain of fear growing in their faces and their eyes never leaving the threatening dirks of the tribesmen.

Mallonee ordered, "Bind them—and quickly." He turned to where Pansy Merigay was white-faced and yammering against the wall. "You're got rope here?" he demanded. She stared at him, and he slapped his hand down on her shoulder and shook her until the hair fell down around her face. "Rope!" he said angrily. "Rope to tie up these men. Where is it?"

She ducked her head and then turned and ran into the kitchen and came back quickly with a coil of weather-blackened Manila. He tossed it across to Tahonkee and the Cherokee grunted and began to chop short lengths off it with his knife.

"Put them in there," Mallonee said crisply, and pointed to the room opposite the kitchen. "And drag this one out of the house when you get through with them."

He swung himself back up into the loft. Melissa was on her feet, swaying a little, but holding herself erect with one hand braced against a rafter of the roof. Her dress was torn away at the shoulder and her black hair was down so that it was like a veil around her face. Even in the dim light he could see that she was young—and very beautiful—and he found time to wonder how a woman like her had ever found her way to such a place.

"It's all right," he said. "It's all over now."

He started to move forward and take her arm, but she shrank back with a cry of fear and her hand went up to her mouth as if she was forcing back the terror that was in her.

"Don't be afraid," he said. His mouth twisted a little as he looked at her. "I won't hurt you. I won't let anyone hurt you."

He didn't want her to go downstairs, not with Keltin's body broken and bloody on the floor, and the tribesmen a crew of devils as they tied the swampers and hustled them into the other room. He looked around, but the attic was bare of anything that could have served as a chair. There was a pallet of blankets and straw at one end, and he judged that she'd been hiding there when Keltin came up and found her. He jerked up the two blankets and kicked the straw up into a pile and put the blankets back over it and turned back to her again.

"Try this for a while. You'll fall if you keep trying to stand up."

She looked at him, saying nothing. Then she nodded and pushed herself away from the rafter and came across the room to where he was standing.

She was so small and young and helpless that he could feel his emotions twisting inside of him in a way he hadn't known before—a way he didn't like. "Sit down there," he said almost brusquely. "Stretch out if you want to. I'm going to get you a drink of something to settle your nerves."

He went back to the trap door and caught a glimpse of the girl Pansy and called down to her. "Draw two cups of whisky," he ordered her, "and hand them up here. And step smart about it."

She hurried away, and was back almost at once with the two brimming tin cups. She stood on tiptoe to reach them to him, and he bent down through the trap door for them and saw that her face was white and strained and almost ashamed.

"That woman—" She hesitated as if she was afraid to go on. "Is she all right up there?"

"She's all right," he said grimly. "But she'd have been a damn sight better if you hadn't told Keltin where to find her."

"I didn't aim to," she said huskily. "She was real kind about Jobe, bandagin' him up an' helpin' me with him after he was burnt. But I couldn't do nothin' else when Burr asked me point blank. I'm scared of him—" She caught herself quickly and her eyes flicked down to Keltin's body and then back again. "I was always scared of him."

He carried the two cups of whisky across to the pallet and handed one to Melissa. She sipped it, shuddering a little, and then tightened her grip on the handle and took a draught that lowered the level in the cup a good inch and a half. She let her breath escape in a long, shuddering sigh and turned her head to look at him again.

"I owe you so much," she said shakily. "If you hadn't—if you hadn't happened to be here—"

"I'm Dale Mallonee," he told her. "I'm on my way to Springfield, up in Missouri."

"Springfield?" Her head came up in surprise and she put the cup down on the floor beside her, carefully. "I'm going to Springfield, too," she said; "if I can get there. I'm going to Springfield to try to find my husband."

"To try to find him?" There was more mystery than one about this dark-haired woman.

"He ran away," she explained wearily. "He was the youngest son, and he was always wild, even after we were married. He killed a man over a card game back in Kentucky, and then he ran away and his father disowned him."

"He was a McCutcheon?"

She nodded, her head drooping a little on her shoulders as if she had come almost to the end of her strength.

"Jeff McCutcheon." There was a sudden bitterness in her voice. "My own people were all gone, and after he ran away I had to live with the McCutcheons." Her head came up and she stared at Mallonee defiantly. "Live with them month after month—" She caught herself, biting her lip and shaking her head as if to bite off the rising resentment that was in her voice.

"And you think he's in Springfield?"

"He wrote me once. He'd found something new, something big, out there in Missouri, and if I'd come out and join him—" She shook her head again, this time in a puzzled bewilderment. "But I don't know what happened then. I answered his letter and told him I'd come and asked him to send me enough money for the trip. But the letter came back with a note scrawled on the back that said he wasn't there any more. They didn't know where he'd gone!"

"But you started out after him, anyway?"

"I'm a fool, I guess, but I still love him—and I begged his brother until he said if I'd get out and leave him alone he'd give me five thousand dollars to make a new start, or hunt for Jeff or do whatever I wanted to do. But he said we mustn't ever come back to Kentucky. They wanted to wash their hands of us and close the books on the whole affair."

"Good God!" he said. "Don't you know there's not a swamper in this house who wouldn't cut your throat for five thousand dollars?"

"I don't have it here," Melissa said. "Not all of it, anyway. Jeff's brother wanted to be so sure I'd really leave that he arranged for the packet captain to give me five hundred dollars when he set me ashore here—and the rest of it's been sent to the Missouri State Bank in Springfield. It's not mine until I get there."

He lifted his tin cup and let the whisky bite into him and tried to think about what she'd told him. Her story could be true, but it was just as possible that it was a pack of lies and she had made up her mind to get something out of him. He looked at her again, at the gypsy face and the nymph-slim body that was like a strain of passionate challenging music. He suddenly decided that whatever she wanted wouldn't be too much to pay for the chance of knowing her better. Much better …

"Why don't you go to Springfield with me?" he said abruptly.

She didn't answer him for a minute, but her eyes studied him and from the way they changed as she looked at him he could tell that she knew exactly what he was thinking and she was making up her mind whether the game was worth it. He felt his fingernails biting into the palms of his hands and his breath was suddenly quick and uneven as he waited for her decision.

She laughed then, a laugh with no lightness or gaiety in it, as if she were laughing at herself, jeering at her own doubts and her own hesitancy.

"Why, that would be lovely, Mr. Mallonee." Her voice had the defiance in it he'd heard in men's voices when they tossed their last dollar down on a gaming table. "If you're not afraid that I'll compromise you."

"You'll not compromise me," he said gruffly. "We'll ride out of here in the morning."

"In the morning, then."

Her eyes went to the trap door, and he knew, with a sudden compassion and understanding, that she had come to the limit of her endurance and her courage. He got to his feet and took a last, long look at her.

"I'll go down to my men now," he said, "but I'll see you tomorrow."

"Most certainly tomorrow," she agreed. "And thank you, Mr. Mallonee."

He nodded and turned away, but he knew she wasn't thanking him for agreeing to take her to Springfield. He could feel her eyes following him, but he kept his back turned as he crossed the floor and worked his way through the trap door and down to the ladder and into the room below.

It would have been hard not to stop and go back to her, if he had let himself look at her again.

CHAPTER THREE

THEY HAD BEEN five days on the road, and yet Melissa knew as little of the affairs that took Dale Mallonee to Missouri as she had known in the moment when he first burst into the loft of Merigay's Tavern. She had thought then that he was simple, a man of action, plain and open. But there was a complexity in him. He thought swiftly, went far beyond her own thoughts, and reached conclusions and reactions that baffled her. And when the mood struck him, he could be as taciturn and uncommunicative as one of his own Indians.

On the fifth day he had sent Tahchee, who seemed to be his favorite, and the short, wide-chested Cherokee that he called Oconto, to ride a mile ahead of the rest. She wondered, for they were not a military column and he had taken no such precaution on the days before. She caught sight of Tahchee and Oconto only now and then, for the trail they'd followed from Litchfield Landing had taken them up out of the flat river bottomlands and for two days they had ridden through a serried, heavily timbered country of high hills and narrow valleys. From a crest, she could see the hills and the valleys for miles ahead, the hills blue-gray and the valleys green with spring. But if Tahchee and Oconto had ridden down into a valley not half a mile away they would be hidden utterly.

She had been riding alone that afternoon, perhaps a hundred yards in advance of Mallonee and the others, when he quickened his horse's pace and came up beside her.

"That last range of hills up ahead—" he waved his arm toward a stratum of ridges some five miles away—"is the boundary between Missouri and Arkansas. When we reach it, we'll not be much more than seventy miles from Springfield—but I think we'll have trouble somewhere between here and there."

"Trouble?" She turned in her saddle. Her knee brushed the repeating pistol holstered at her saddle bow and she pushed it aside. "Between here and those cliffs, you mean? But there's nothing that I can see to give us trouble."

"It might be a damn sight better if we could see it. That's why I sent Oconto and Tahchee on ahead. I think it's about ten to one we're going to be bushwhacked, Melissa, and if that does happen I want you to turn and ride back the way we've come as fast as the Lord will let you."

"Bushwhacked!" The word had an ugly sound, the sound of guerrilla warfare. "Who'd want to bushwhack us, Dale Mallonee?"

"No one you know—and no one I want you to know, as far as that goes." He lifted his head and his eyes raked the terrain ahead. Then he turned back to her and kneed his horse in a little closer to her. "Since you're likely to be in it," he said casually, "it's no more than right for you to know a little about it. I'll tell you a story, Melissa…

"When I came back from war in Mexico—seven years ago, in 1848—I'd had two years of it with Worth's Dragoons and I wanted to go home and settle down. I came back through New Orleans, where I met a man named Dorsey Wilcox. He'd had army service, as I had had, and between the two of us we had a little capital. We went back to Colquitt and opened a cotton factoring office there. My family had owned a plantation there until we lost it to the moneylenders—and I had friends and the business did well. But two years ago Wilcox ran away with a young married woman named Charlotte Sherwood and when they left they took every last dollar he and I both had along with them. They left me without a penny."

"Ah," she said, "I know how that is."

"Well, I was bankrupt, and I finally wound up in the Cherokee village where I'd played when I was a boy. But a month ago I got word of Wilcox."

"In Springfield?"

"In Springfield. The story was that he still had young Charlotte with him, and somehow or other he'd come to be a power in the country. Mills and stage lines and farms and shares in a bank and business buildings and sawmills—he had them all."

"And you had financed them for him."

"Damned if I hadn't! I packed the records of the factoring business on a pack mule, so I could prove my case if I had to go into court in Missouri, and gathered up these boys for a body-guard—" his gesture embraced the four Cherokees riding behind them—"and started for Missouri. There was another man with us at the start, a no-account named Harlin Sills, who'd worked for us and claimed Wilcox owed him money, too. He wanted to come along, and since there wasn't any good way to refuse him, he joined us." His voice changed, turned so deadly and cold that it frightened her. "And if I ever see him again—I'll kill him!"

"But where is he?"

"That's the reason I think we're going to get bushwhacked, Melissa. I was out of my head with the fever for a week, just out-side of Vicksburg, and when I came to I found Sills had taken the pack mule and the records and run away. I found trace of him as we came north, and there's no doubt in my mind that he decided it would be more profitable to go on ahead and sell the records to Wilcox than it was to stay with me and take a chance on getting nothing."

"He should be killed!" Illogically, she found herself tak-ing up arms for Mallonee as fiercely as if it had been her own quarrel. "But, Mallonee—what has this to do with ambushing or bushwhacking."

"You don't know Dorsey Wilcox. With or without the records I can still ruin him wherever I find him—and he's the man to know that, too. He'll buy the records from Sills right away—and probably cut his throat to make sure he doesn't talk—but he'll take steps to see that I never get to Springfield, too. There's no doubt of that. He's got money and he's probably got men, and he'll use them both to try to stop us before we get much closer. As I figure it, there's been just about time enough for Sills to have reached Springfield and told his story, and for Wilcox to have made up a party and started them south to meet us. If I'm not wrong, we'll run into each other somewhere right near the state line—and that's the state line I pointed out to you a few minutes ago."

She caught her breath and looked at the line of hills ahead. She shuddered, feeling the blood drain out of her face. She could feel fear clutching at her like a ghostly hand.

"But then let's turn aside! Let's go back! For God's sake, Mallonee, we aren't going to ride right into their hands!"

"Easy now." He reached over and patted her shoulder and she jerked away and glared at him, hating him for having brought her into this danger. "There aren't any better woodsmen—or fighters, either—than Tahchee and Oconto. I think they'll smell them out before we run into them." His face hardened. "But whether they do or not, I've got to get to Springfield and find Wilcox. There's no other trail through these mountains except the one we're on."

"So we're all to be killed to get your money back for you!"

She was raging with the unreasoning fury that terror brings, and she jerked up her arm with the idea of lashing him with her riding whip.

It hissed like a snake as she struck at him, but before it reached him his arm shot out and his left hand was an iron clamp around her wrist. His other hand twisted the whip out of her hand.

"That was a damned dangerous thing for you to do." There were white lines around the corners of his mouth, and his eyes blazed. "I've had a hard enough time keeping my hands off of you ever since we started. One more invitation like that, and I'll—"

"An invitation?" she stormed at him, and she knew that her face was suddenly as red as fire. "Why, I wouldn't let you touch me if you were—"

His eyes stopped her.

"I'm sorry, Mallonee," she said. "Sorry for what I did and sorry for what I said. We've both been acting like children."

She saw lines of laughter gather suddenly at the corners of his eyes, and before she realized what he was doing he had dropped her wrist and his arm was around her shoulders and he was kissing her as a woman dreams of being kissed when she is restless and hungry with unsatisfied desires. He let her go, and even though the earth was whirling and the points of her breasts were suddenly hard and hot against her bodice, she saw that the laughter had gone out of his face, erased by something fierce and demanding.

"But children do grow up," he said curtly. "And then they aren't satisfied with games and waiting and playing pretend."

He pulled himself up straight in his saddle and tossed her whip across to her, and she saw his hands tighten on the reins as he prepared to whirl his horse and go. Her throat was tight and swollen and she had a wild impulse to bury her head in her hands and laugh and cry all at the same time. She let the whip fall to the ground as she tried to lean forward and catch Mallonee's bridle rein.

"Wait, Mallonee," she gasped breathlessly. "We don't have to play games! We don't have to—"

"Why, by hell, then—" He whirled the horse sharply back toward her—and just in that instant they heard the sudden sharp stabbing of rifle fire ahead and Tahchee's voice rising in a savage scream that was blotted out in a second volley of slashing reports.

For the space of a heartbeat they were frozen into images of paralyzed surprise, and then Kahena whooped behind them and Atahulla's shout joined his and Mallonee was pulling his horse around while his voice thundered at her.

"Ride to the rear! And ride as if the devil chased you!"

Melissa's horse reared and by the time she had him under control, the Cherokees had swept by her and were racing toward the sound of the guns with Mallonee half a length in the lead, his arm rising and falling as his whip lashed the straining flanks of his stallion.

"Mallonee!" she screamed. "Wait, Mallonee—"

And then she was suddenly ashamed and put her horse straight at the sharp-rising ridge that edged the trail and on up into the shelter of the timber. She turned him then, not to the rear but in the direction that Mallonee and the others had taken. She forced him into a driving gallop, low tree limbs threatening to sweep her out of the saddle and the thorn bushes tearing at her riding skirt as she raced after them, hidden by the trees.

It seemed to her that the firing was heavier up ahead, and she urged the horse forward recklessly, swaying with him as he slipped and slid on the carpet of small rocks that covered the slope, crouching and then rising in her saddle as he cleared an unsuspected gully or the fallen bole of a tree. At least, she thought grimly, Kentucky had been good to her in that, for she'd ridden before she had her first lesson in her ABC's. The timber began to thin out before her, the heavy growth of trees giving way to a scattering of saplings and undergrowth, and she pulled the horse down to a trot.

She could see the smoke from the guns now—and smell it, when the wind turned toward her—and not more than two hundred feet away she could make out Mallonee and his band of tribesmen. They had left their horses and were crashing into the shelter of the timber on the opposite side of the trail. Even though the growth almost hid them, she could see that they had spread out in a rough semicircle as they worked their way toward an exposed cliff overlooking the trail. There was no one in sight upon it, but she could make out horses tethered in a thicket below, and gunsmoke came up in little wisps and clouds from the barricade of trees that edged the trail.

Sunlight glinted on a rifle barrel, and there was a puff of gun-smoke high up on the hill above the cliff edge where the attackers were hidden. For an instant she thought they had thrown out a flank to catch Mallonee and his men between two fires. But then—in the instant she saw the gun and the puff of smoke—a sniper who'd been hidden at the edge of the cliff stumbled out into the open with his hands clawing at his chest. He tumbled backward, in a grotesque, awkward dance. His legs collapsed beneath him and he sprawled flat on his back with his face turned up toward the sky. His hands, stiff and rigid now, were still clenched in the shirt front.

"Oh, Tahchee—do it again!" She whispered to herself in a sudden tingling burst of exultation as she realized the identity of the marksman high up on the hill. Tahchee or Oconto, or perhaps even both of them. Somehow, they'd managed to break away from the first skirmish that had been touched off when they rode into range of the guns hidden on the cliff top. And from there they'd worked their way up into the timber above the cliff so that they could rake it with hail of fire while Mallonee and the others worked in close enough to come to grips with the enemy.

The thunder of the guns crashed and ricocheted from wall to wall in the narrow pass, until it was impossible to separate the sound of one gun from another. But Melissa saw two puffs of smoke not twenty feet apart bloom on the face of the hill again, and a stir of movement in the trees told her the bullets had found their mark.

The stir widened, grew into a spreading ripple of suddenly revealed action as two men, and then a third, bolted up out of the cover of the trees and then raced across the cliff top to dive into the tangle of underbrush and timber that edged it on the farther side. High as she was above them, it was easy to follow their passage through the sudden swaying and pitching of the low brush they pushed aside as they ran. They went crashing down the farther slope, there was a moment when she thought she had lost them, and then three horses burst out into the trail, with the fugitives bent low in the saddle, and raced north up the trail, away from the fighting, with their riders whipping and spurring wildly.

She knew that Mallonee could not have seen them, and she whirled back with some wild idea of crying out to him, but she realized that her voice could not possibly carry against the hammering of the guns. But he and his men had gained ground while she was watching the three deserters. He was on the end of the semicircle nearest the trail, and she gasped as she realized that he and his men had fought and ducked and dodged their way forward until they were not much more than forty feet from the bare rim of the cliff top.

She saw Mallonee raise himself cautiously to get his bearings, and then his head turned slowly as his eyes probed through the brush and timber, picking out the positions of the four Cherokees who completed the halfcircle. Two of them she could see; they were as close to the cliff top as Mallonee himself. The others were out of sight, but Mallonee must have seen them and been satisfied with their positions, for she heard his voice go up in a high-pitched, staccato signal that was like the yelping of a wolf. All around the arc the call answered him and in the same instant all five plunged toward the naked rock of the cliff, rifles thrust forward and voices squalling.

The trees rimming the cliff top seemed to spout gray volcanoes of smoke as the guerrillas fired frantically in an effort to beat back the charge. But even the best marksmanship was unsure in that maze of timbered underbrush, and before they could load again, Mallonee and the Indians were on them, firing as they closed in and then clubbing their guns and hauling the half-dozen defenders back and out into the open. Locked in a furious, wildly straining coil of violence, the two groups became one, with knives flashing and gunbutts swinging like flails as the fight surged back and forth across the naked rock.

It was horrifying, but she could no more have torn her eyes away from it than she could have ripped out her own heart. The palms of her hands were covered with sweat and when she wrung them against each other she realized they were trembling. A hard ball of panic throbbed in her throat, choking her, and yet she would have given anything if she could have been beside Mallonee.

A spine-tingling whoop of triumph skirled up like a mad bugle call and she saw Tahonkee and one of the guerrillas struggling on the very edge of the cliff. The Indian's knife flashed white in the sunlight, and sank deep into the other's breast, and then the guerrilla was down and the Cherokee's knife was bright again. With a shock that was almost nausea, she realized that he was tearing the scalp from his victim's head, the long knife in one hand and the bloody clot of hair and flesh in the other. He dived back into the whirl of bodies, and in the same instant Mallonee and another of the guerrillas seemed to burst out of the crush. Mallonee was empty-handed, and he had thrown up both arms to guard his head against the furious blows the guerrilla was raining down upon him with the butt of a clubbed musket.

The action was almost too swift to follow, but she saw Mallonee forced back to the edge of the cliff, saw him duck and try to whirl aside, and then the clubbed gun broke through his guard and his head jerked back and he was pinwheeling down the cliff to the trail thirty feet below, his body turning and jerking—and then suddenly still and silent in the grass at the edge of the trail.

She had set the spurs to her horse almost without realizing it, and she was halfway down the slope when Mallonee's body crashed into the ground. Some instinct made her fumble for the pistol swinging from the pommel of the saddle, and it was in her hand as her horse plunged down into the trail with the rocks flying under his hoofs as he fought desperately to keep his feet. Mallonee was almost two hundred feet away, and as she lashed the horse toward him she saw another horse and rider explode out of the thicket where she had seen the three deserters.

He was mounted on a magnificent bay mare, and her heart seemed to stop as she realized that his pounding charge would bring him to Mallonee while she was still a hundred feet away. She jerked up the pistol and began to fire wildly, the pounding gallop of her mount barring even the faintest possibility of accuracy. The first two shots went wild. He was no more than a score of feet from Mallonee, the clubbed gun swinging like a cavalry saber. She threw herself back in the saddle, checking her mount so abruptly that he came straight up, his hind legs dancing on the ground and his front feet pawing the air. For an instant they seemed to hang there, frozen and motionless, and in that instant she put a bullet straight into the guerrilla's shoulder.

He lurched in his saddle and the musket went spinning down to the ground. His horse swerved, the pounding hoofs missing Mallonee's head by no more than a hair. She fired again as her horse came down and the bay mare screamed and whirled away, blood streaming from its shoulder. The rider was weaving forward over the saddle horn, as the mare's hoofs flung stones behind her. The two of them swept out of sight around a bend in the trail, and she lashed herself forward and flung herself out of the saddle beside Mallonee's body just as Tahonkee and Atahulla came rocketing down the sheer face of the cliff in the turmoil of a self-made avalanche.

Takonkee threw himself on his knees beside Mallonee, and she caught her breath as his fingertips pushed Mallonee's eyelids open. For an instant, her heart turned into stone and then the eyes moved, looking up at Tahonkee, and Mallonee tried to lift his head.

"He good," Tahonkee grunted. "Not hurt too much." He turned his head to look at her, the obsidian eyes black and inscrutable. "All gone," he said. He jerked his head toward the cliff. "All gone up there. All right, now."

She nodded numbly, feeling the trembling start in her shoulders and run across her body.

"All right," the Cherokee had said. "All right, now."

But nothing could ever be right again—for the guerrilla who had ridden the bay mare, the hired bravo who had tried to assassinate them all was her husband, Jeffrey McCutcheon!

CHAPTER FOUR

Jeffrey McCutcheon swung wide around Springfield and took the Old Cabin Road that would bring him back to Dorsey Wilcox's farm. He'd been swinging wide around Springfield for more than a month now, ever since that homesteader from Illinois found him going through his trunk that night at Tiff's Wagon Yard and Jeff had had to kill him. The homesteader's brother had seen him do it, and his wife and two of his children, too. But they hadn't known who he was, so that if he stayed out of sight there'd been no way they could identify him.

They were still in Springfield, hoping to see him again, but they'd have to be pushing on to Kansas soon. Once they were gone, there wouldn't be anyone who knew except Dorsey Wilcox—and Dorsey's wife, Charlotte, of course. But Dorsey wouldn't talk. Anyway, he didn't think he would, even though he did use what he knew to crack a whip over Jeffrey's head whenever he had a particularly dirty job he wanted done.

The ambushing of Mallonee and his Indians had been one of those jobs. Not that Jeff gave a damn about Mallonee one way or the other. If he was—as Dorsey said he was—a former partner with a grudge, and he wanted to kill Dorsey or ruin him financially, Jeff didn't mind giving Dorsey a hand in getting rid of him.

But he hadn't expected to find Melissa with him!

His belly churned every time he thought about that. He was positive she hadn't recognized him, and he hadn't known her until the very last, after she'd shot him and was bringing her gun down for the second shot that took his mare in the shoulder. And he couldn't go back then. Every man he had was dead except the three deserters, and those damned Indians of Mallonee's were so wildeyed and trigger-hot that they'd have had a bullet in his guts and his scalp off before he could open his mouth.

No, there wasn't any way he could have gone to her. But what was she doing with Mallonee? She hadn't been with them when they left Mississippi—Sills would have mentioned her when he brought the stolen cotton-factor records in to Wilcox. She must have joined them somewhere along the road. But what was she doing on the road to Springfield, anyway? Jeff had written and asked her to come to him—but he'd never heard from her, and he'd made up his mind that she was through with him.

But maybe she was coming to Springfield to try to find him! He felt himself grow warm at the thought of her and then the glow vanished abruptly as he realized that Dorsey would kill her just as ruthlessly as he'd kill the Indians, if they all came into Springfield with Mallonee.

And he didn't want anything to happen to her! By hell, he wasn't going to let anything happen to her ....

Wilcox's wife, Charlotte, was standing on the veranda of the farmhouse when he rode up the lane. She was such a damned handsome woman that the sight of her drove Melissa out of his mind. A slim blonde, she had long legs, blue eyes ringed in coal-black lashes, and the most beautiful, slim-fingered hands he'd ever seen on a woman. A calculating bitch, though, and as sensuously amoral as a cat. There'd been more times than one during the month he'd been hiding out on the farm when he'd come within an ace of getting her into his hands, but she'd always slipped free at the last moment.

It was almost sundown, and the two-story white columns that ran the full height of the double veranda cast their shadows across her, but they couldn't hide the honey-gold of her hair, or the red mouth smiling at him, or the way the soft wind plastered her green dress against her. A colored groom came running up to take his horse, and he threw him the reins and came down out of the saddle, wincing a little with the pain of the bullet wound in his shoulder. It was still stiff and sore, but the swelling was gone, thanks to that fact that he'd stopped at an isolated cabin down on the lower James and paid an old ridge runner to dig out the bullet and bind the wound.

"Ah, Jeff—the conquering hero's come home again!"

She had a lovely voice, though there was nearly always an undertone of teasing mockery in it when she was talking to him. She dropped him a mock curtsy and he went up the steps with his boot heels clicking on the wide planks. He put his arm around her waist and kissed her hard on the lips in a way that he'd known to leave other women eager and breathless.

But Charlotte was far from breathless. She'd let herself come hard against him—thighs, breasts and lips—but when he raised his head she was still cool, completely self-possessed. Her hand came up, lovely long fingers touching the black cotton sling that supported his arm.

"You've been wounded!" she said sharply. She stared at him with her eyes deep and intent in the black rim of lashes. "It didn't go well, then? You didn't get rid of Mallonee!"

"Mallonee damned near got rid of me," he said dryly.

The thought of Melissa came back hard then, and he suddenly wanted her there in his arms instead of this yellow-haired woman who was another man's wife.

"Let's go inside and have a drink," he said gruffly. "I'm tired as all hell."

She had wit enough not to badger him, and nodded in quick agreement. She made a little sound of sympathy and slipped her arm around his waist as they walked across the veranda and into the library, where a cheerful fire was burning on the hearth. She poured brandy from a decanter, handed him a glass, and then sat down on the sofa beside him with her own glass cradled in her hand.

"Tell me now," she said. The laughter had gone out of her face, and there was a disquiet there that might almost have been fear, although he could see no reason for that.

He took a deep draught out of his glass and let his eyes study her unsmilingly. He wanted to tell it so that she'd get just the impression he wanted her to have. And after it was told, he had more that he wanted to say to her, too. It was a long-shot gamble, the longest he'd ever taken in his life, and if he made a mistake neither his life nor Melissa's would be worth more than the price of a charge of powder.

"I don't think Dorsey's going to be able to stop Mallonee this time, Charlotte," he said slowly, and he saw her eyes widen in alarm. "He's a hard fighter, and a good one—I'll take oath to that. And he's brought a bodyguard of Indians with him—how many I don't know, but there were enough of them to wipe out all but three of the ten men I took with me, and those three ran away. I think Dorsey's finished, Charlotte."

"But he can't be!" She slapped her glass down on the marble-topped table and her lips stiffened angrily. "Once you've warned Dorsey, he can get more men. Or he can get out of the country and leave someone here who can handle Mallonee."

"I'm not so damned sure I'm going to warn Dorsey," he told her.

Her eyes widened and she shook her head as if to say she couldn't have heard him right. "But you've got to warn him," she protested. "If you don't I will, and then—"

"And then he'll see that I'm shot in the back before this time tomorrow," he agreed. "But that won't keep Mallonee from killing him."

He leaned forward and put his hand on her arm and let his fingers bite in a little. "I'm going to tell you something, Charlotte, and if you're as smart as I think you are, you're going to listen. Almost two months ago I wrote to my wife Melissa, in Kentucky, and asked her to come out here and join me. I didn't hear from her. But she's with Mallonee now—she's the one who gave me this hole in the shoulder!"

"She knew you? And she tried to kill you?"

"She didn't know me—she couldn't have known me. But I recognized her. If she comes into Springfield with Mallonee and his Indians and Dorsey's ready and waiting for them, he'll kill her just as he'll try to kill the rest of them. I'm not going to have that, Charlotte."

"You're still in love with her, then! You want her enough to buck Dorsey to try to save her!" She leaned back, relaxing a little, and the half-jeering note of laughter came back into her voice. "Don't you know that all Dorsey has to do to get rid of you is go to the authorities and tell them that he saw you the night you killed that immigrant in the wagon yard? He'd do that without thinking twice."

"That's exactly what I do know," he agreed grimly. "And that's another reason I'm not going to lift a hand to keep Mallonee from killing him. But you're overlooking your part in this thing, Charlotte." He tightened his grip on her arm again to compel her attention. "You'd be a damn sight better off if Dorsey were dead, too."

"Better off?" She jerked her arm away and glared at him with eyes that snapped. "Why, if Dorsey was dead I'd be nothing! I'd have nothing! I'd be walking the streets—"

"There aren't many wealthy widows walking the streets," he said dryly. "Not in Missouri and not anywhere else."

"Wealthy widows—" she broke off the words and stared at him. "So that's what you've got in mind! I'm to keep quiet and help you save your Melissa, and my reward is to be that I'll be Dorsey's wealthy widow!" She bit her lower lip, eyes narrowed in concentration and fingers beating out a sharp tattoo on the table. "But I don't think it would work out that way, Jeff."

"Why, hell—it can't work out any other way!" He was insistent now, leaning forward and driving his argument home with all the persuasion he could muster. "Forget any nonsense you might have in your head about loyalty to Dorsey, and think about your situation the way it really is for a minute. For the last six months Dorsey hasn't been out here at the farm with you more than two or three nights out of the month, has he?"

"He's been busy." Charlotte shrugged her shoulders. "And it's a long ride out here."

"He's been busy, right enough." He laughed, and saw the quick flush of anger flood her cheeks. "He's been busy with a red-headed little vixen called Jean Bruillot who came in here with a troupe of traveling players last fall and stayed behind when they went on to Memphis. And Jean Bruillot knows a damn sight more about handling Dorsey than you do, Charlotte. She's got him just like that—" He held out his open hand and then closed the fingers sharply down into a hard fist to symbolize his point. "And one of these days she's going to turn you out and she'll be the new Mrs. Dorsey Wilcox—if you're damned fool enough to turn down this chance."

"So that's it! I thought he must have someone—" She slapped her hand down hard on the table and then got to her feet and began to pace up and down the room, her hands clasped behind her and her head bent a little as she weighed the pros and cons of it. She stopped suddenly, whirled, and faced him with narrowed eyes. "You're not lying to me, Jeffrey McCutcheon?"

"About our Jeanie with the bright red hair? It's as true as gospel, Charlotte. It's common talk in Springfield."

"Ah—so?" Her face hardened and her mouth became a thin, tight line. "And what's your stake in all this, Jeff? Safety for Melissa? It's not like you to be satisfied with no more than that."

"I didn't say there was no more than that." He picked up the drink she'd mixed for him and let her stare while he drained the glass. "There's much more than that, as a matter of fact. First, I assure Melissa's safety and get her back again. Second, I wipe out the threat Dorsey's holding over my head. And third, my dear Charlotte, is that you share a part of what you'll inherit from Dorsey—a third of it, maybe—as a sign of your deep gratitude to me and as an assurance that I'll take Melissa and go away and never tell anyone you had a hand in this."

"Yes," she nodded her head slowly, "you would want that, wouldn't you? And you've told me all of it now? There's nothing else that you're holding back?"

"What else could there be?" He was more at ease now. The shot about Jean Bruillot had hit her hard; she hadn't been able to disguise that. "We'll both save our skins and we'll never be able to do it this easily—and let somebody else take the blame for it. You'd be a fool not to agree, Charlotte."

"Oh, I'm not a fool, Jeff." She came back and sat down beside him and her hand came out and turned his hand palm upward and closed down tight around it. "I won't deny that I may regret Melissa a little, but that's neither here nor there—and she isn't here yet, anyway. Now, how do you propose to do all this?"

"That's simple enough." He tightened the hold of his hand on hers and thought about the night that was coming down on them and the idea that she was right about Melissa not being there. "I'll send Dorsey a note—you'll have to write it for me since my right arm's too sore—and tell him that Mallonee's wiped out and he's got nothing more to worry about. After that—why, after that, my dear, we can relax out here in the country, enjoy each other's company, and wait for Mallonee to settle our affairs for us."

"Why, yes," she agreed, and there was a sudden trace of excitement in her voice. "Why, yes, we can do that. Shall I write the note for you now?"

"We'll write it now," he said, and she went across the room to the glass-fronted secretary and produced pen and ink and paper.

"Dear Dorsey—" he dictated. "The business I went to attend to has been completed in full. The parties I met will be unable to carry out any of their plans."

He got up and crossed the room so that he could look down over her shoulder. The carefully guarded phrases were there, just as he had given them to her. "You'd better put a postscript on it to say that you're writing because I've got a bullet in my arm," he suggested, and she added that and sanded it and then waved the paper in the air to shake the sand away.

"I'll get one of the grooms and send him into town with it now," she suggested. She stood up and started for the door, and he went back to the decanter and poured himself another drink.

"You do that," he agreed. "I'll get into some clean clothes." He twisted the drink in his hands, struck by a sudden idea that hadn't occurred to him before. "Do you think the note will do it? You don't think Dorsey will question it if I don't go in and give him a report in person?"

"Oh, no!" Her rejection of the idea was quick. "He'd never expect you to come into Springfield while those immigrants are still looking for you."

She opened the door and was halfway through it when she hesitated and turned back to him. "Jeff," she said softly, "what sort of a looking woman is Melissa, anyway?"

"Melissa? Why, Melissa's a damned beautiful woman. She's— let's see now—she was twenty-three years old this spring. Very black hair and dark eyes and a figure—" He hesitated, remembering it. "A very slim, lovely figure. But what's this sudden interest in Melissa?"

"Why, Jeff—" She tilted her head to one side, her eyes laughing and her lips coyly pursed. "Don't you know a woman is always curious about her rivals?"

It seemed to him for a moment that the old undertone of mockery had come back into her voice and that she was laughing at him. But he couldn't be sure, and she had slipped out into the hall and closed the door before he could answer her.

CHAPTER FIVE

"THE MAN'S A FOOL," Charlotte thought scornfully as the library door closed behind her. "A wealthy widow—" Her lips curled contemptuously.

She slipped into the little drawing room directly across the hall and pulled the door closed until there was only a narrow open slit through which she could watch the hall. In a moment she saw Jeff come out of the library, the cavalry jacket and the orange scarf thrown across his arm, and go stamping up the stairs to his room. When she was sure he was gone, she ran back across the hall and sat down at the secretary again.

The point was, she told herself, that Jeff didn't know she wasn't Dorsey Wilcox's wife, even though she'd pretended to be ever since they came to Missouri. But she couldn't be Dorsey's wife—not while Lin Sherwood was still alive in Mississippi, and still Charlotte's husband. She'd never mustered up the courage to sue for divorce; that would mean serving papers on him and once he knew where she was—she shuddered, thinking about it—he'd be in Springfield as fast as a good horse could bring him. And he'd have had a gun in each hand. One for her—and the other for Dorsey.

That was where Jeff had made his mistake. She felt derision rising in her as she thought of him sitting there, so solemn and so wise, telling her in all seriousness that if Mallonee killed Dorsey she'd be a wealthy widow.

She got up and went across to the fireplace and tore up the note she'd written for Jeff and dropped it into the fire. Back at the desk, she spread fresh paper before her and began to write to Dorsey. Ten to one, she thought savagely, Mallonee's going to send Jeff's precious Melissa in ahead to scout the land for him. But if Dorsey knows Mallonee's still alive, and if he's on the lookout for her—

She told him all of it, all except the fact that Jeff had refused to warn him, had intended to betray him. It wouldn't have helped any with Mallonee, and there might come a time when that information would be valuable to her as something she could hold over Jeffrey McCutcheon's reckless head. A sharp tingling went up her spine as it occurred to her that she might even let Jeff dispose of the red-headed Jean Bruillot. There'd be a certain poetic justice in that—and with what she knew about him now, he couldn't refuse her.

She sanded the letter, sealed it, and called for a groom. "You're to take a fast horse and get this into Springfield as soon as you can," she said curtly. "And it's to go to no one except Mr. Wilcox. You understand that, do you? Put it in Mr. Wilcox's hand!"

She dismissed him and poured a drink from the decanter and tried to think of anything she might have overlooked. There was only one thing—unlikely, but a risk nevertheless. After the first note was written, Jeff had begun to worry about whether Dorsey would believe him unless he went into Springfield and reported in person. She'd tried to laugh the idea away, but he was a reckless fool, as unpredictable as the wind. And she didn't want him talking to Dorsey now. At best, it would be his spoken lie against her note; and at worst—if he found out she'd tricked him—it wouldn't be beyond him to get back to the farm and put a bullet between her eyes. No—she had to keep him with her.

Charlotte went upstairs to her room and stripped off her clothes. In front of the tall pier glass, naked except for her high-heeled slippers, she lifted her arms and saw the sharp line of her breasts tighten and her waist go willow-slim above rounded hips and thighs. She turned slowly, knowing secretly that no man, least of all Jeffrey McCutcheon, would refuse the gift.

There was a satin lounging robe in her closet, and she put it on and pulled the belt tight around her waist. Then she opened the door and ran across the hall to the door of Jeff's room. She could hear him whistling as he moved about the room, and she opened the door without knocking and slipped inside. Evidently he'd had one of the houseboys come in to shave him and change the bandage on his shoulder, for his face was smooth and the linen pad strapped against his arm was clean and white.

"Jeff!" she said very softly. He whirled and stared at her, and then came across the room in three strides.

"I didn't look for you—" he grinned at her—"so soon."

She damned him silently for the insolence of his words.

"Is it—too soon?"

"My God, no!"

His face lit up and he pulled her over to him. She let her body go tight against him, moving and swaying and pressing into his. He kissed her then, fiercely, almost bitterly, and began to fumble at the fastenings of the cameo brooch that held the top of the lounging robe together.

He did it awkwardly, for he was trying to use his wounded arm. She reached up and loosened the brooch and threw it down as the robe fell open. Her breasts were sharp-pointed, glowing like apples long-warmed in the sun. He caught his breath and whispered something.

She moved back into his arms and nuzzled his neck with her lips and felt the goodness flowing through her.

"Can I stay with you tonight, Jeff?" she said softly, and his arms tightened around her. He lifted her chin, his mouth hard and strong and eager against her lips.

It was answer enough. He wouldn't be riding into Springfield that night—or any other night she didn't want him to. He'd be there with her, as long as she wanted him, and Melissa—his damned Melissa, Charlotte thought savagely—could fend for herself.

CHAPTER SIX

AFTER THEY HAD BEATEN OFF Jeffrey McCutcheon's attack, Melissa and Mallonee and the six Cherokees pulled back into the timber and camped near a jagged ridge in a horseshoe valley. Mallonee's head was bandaged. His left arm was bruised and too stiff to move, but there were no broken bones. He told them they would move on in the morning if there were no renewal of the attack during the night.

"And I don't think there will be, Melissa," Mallonee said reassuringly. She had been pale and quiet—too quiet, he thought—ever since he had opened his eyes and found her kneeling beside him. "If they'd had any more men, they'd have thrown them in right at the start. But they'll be watching for us to ride into Springfield."

"They'll kill you if you ride in there now," she said sharply. Her nerves were like taut wires, but there'd be no release with the image of Jeff's murderous attack in her mind. She tried to sort out her tangled reactions toward him.

She'd loved him when she married him—or perhaps she had only been in love with him. When you loved someone, you had to respect them and admire them, but you could be in love with a handsome face and a ready laugh. When he'd run away, she'd begun to hate him; hate him for abandoning her to a position vulnerable to scorn and gossip and, worse, a condescending and supercilious sympathy. She'd thought she'd never forgive him for that.

Looking back at it now, she wondered if she ever had forgiven him. Maybe the begging and the promises that had finally allowed her to leave Kentucky and hunt for him had not really been motivated by any desire to rejoin him; maybe it had been a screen to hide her need to escape from an intolerable situation.

"It seems so—so much worse than it was before," Melissa told Mallonee unhappily, and then caught herself. It was not her intention to tell Mallonee that the leader of the raiders had been her husband; there would be too much shame in any such admission. Later, if it fell out that her life and Mallonee's were to run together in any permanence and significance....

It's better, in some ways." Mallonee was sitting on the blanket she had spread for them, his eyes narrowed as he stared into the yellowing embers of the evening's cooking fire. "We're still alive, and we can be fairly sure we won't run into any more trouble until we get to Springfield."

"They'll be watching for us."

"They'll be ready for us. There'll be a man and a gun waiting in every spot in town. We'll have death all around us every hour and every minute, but we won't be able to pick it out of the crowd until it's too late."

"But you can't go into a thing like that, Mallonee! You've got to have an even chance."

"The only way we'd have an even chance," he said bitterly, "would be to see inside Dorsey Wilcox's mind and know what sort of trap he has planned for us."

To see inside Dorsey's mind. Melissa thought. That was the solution! "Mallonee!" She leaned forward, her eyes sharp, her body tense. "A woman could learn what's in Wilcox's mind! The right woman could do it. I could."

He turned to look at her with a frown gathering between his eyes and she knew that he had caught the significance of her suggestion.

"You mean you'd go in there and become—intimate—with him, don't you?"

Intimate! Her mind recoiled from the implication of the word. But it would not have to come to that. Her mind clutched fiercely at the doubtful assurance, forcing it to assume the shape and texture of certainty.

"You haven't been intimate with every woman who ever got a concession or a scrap of information from you, have you?" she demanded. "You've seen some who got what they wanted without that?"

He laughed wryly. "More without it than with it, worse luck!" he admitted. "But when you come down to it, there's no reason for you to put your neck into the noose at all. You can ride into Springfield and forget me and go on about finding your husband."

"But I'm not going to! I'm going in ahead, and I'm going to find out what Wilcox has planned. I'm going to help you do what you came up here to do!" She was suddenly breathless and she dropped back on the blanket, averting her eyes from Mallonee and wondering desperately, hopelessly, if her outburst had revealed her as a romantic fool intent upon thrusting herself in where she was not wanted.

"You're an amazing person, Melissa."

"What are you going to do while I go into Springfield?" she demanded. "You can't stay on this trail; you can't be sure Wilcox won't send out another party."

"No, and it wouldn't do for you to come in off this trail anyway," Mallonee agreed. "The man you shot may not even have known that you were a woman. But we can't take a chance on that. You'll have to go in from the east or the west—on a stagecoach, preferably—so there'll be no sign of a connection between us."

"From the east then," her mind accepted the suggestion instantly, "for that's the way I'd naturally come from Kentucky if I'd made the trip overland. Can't we cut northeast from here and strike the stage road from Rolla to Springfield? I can catch a stage and you can wait there till I can send word back to you."

He laughed. "With Tahchee to find the way, we could go from here to Philadelphia and not go ten miles out of our road all the way," he assured her. "We'll strike a little rough country, but we can get over that."

"It's going to take something worse than rough country to bother me after today. I feel like Daniel Boone." She yawned. "A dog-tired Daniel Boone," she admitted. "I'm ready to drop in my tracks. I think I'll go to bed, Mallonee."

She saw the light flare up in his eyes and then fade slowly. She stood up and smiled at him. I'm almost sure, she thought. "Good night, Mallonee," she said.

"Good night," he answered, smiling. "Remember what I told you before."

She waited, wondering.

"You're an amazing person, Melissa."

They struck the stage road some thirty miles east of Springfield, where the hills fanned out into a wide valley with a river running through it. There was a weathered brick house beside the river, two-storied, high-windowed, with a sharply peaked roof. It faced the rutted stage road that snaked down out of the eastern hills, separated from it by a wide lawn where the first grass was pushing up in scattered patches to relieve the cold brown drabness of the earth. The lawn had a scattering of untrimmed trees and neglected shrubbery, a fit setting for the house, with its shutters gone awry at its curtainless windows.

Melissa saw a red-bearded little man, no bigger than a boy, step down off the porch and come swaggering across to them.

He wore a purple shirt and a pair of checkered black and yellow trousers that must have come straight out of a minstrel show. His beard was magnificent, a wild torrent of brick-red hair that spread across his chest and came halfway to his waist. His boots were polished until they shone like mirrors, and he carried a fiddle in one hand and a bow in the other as he stepped spryly toward them.

She stifled a sudden impulse to laugh and when she shot a glance at Mallonee, she saw that he was staring at the little man in blank, unbelieving surprise.

"Light down an' rest yourselves an' bear me company a spell!" the little man began to roar when he was still thirty feet away. "Hain't been no new face round here for better'n a fortnight, an' even then I couldn't draw no better'n a dried-up circuit rider that didn't have no ear for fiddle sawin' an' couldn't a stepped a hoedown if he'd been goin' to be hung for not doin' it. I'm Fiddley Flanders. I'll be plumb proud if you'll jine me an' make free of what little I've got."

Mallonee turned to Melissa, his eyebrows raised in a quizzical question, and she nodded delightedly, her eyes sparkling with anticipation. The strains and tensions of the past week suddenly swept away on the tide of laughter that bubbled up in her throat.

He motioned to the Cherokees to dismount and he and Melissa swung out of their saddles as half a dozen Negroes came scuttling down the lane to take the horses in response to Fiddley's bellow of command.

"I reckon you're strangers hereabouts, ain't you?" Fiddley demanded genially, and Mallonee gave him their names as they shook hands. Then he called up the tribesmen and presented them one by one as Fiddley's eyes widened in joyous incredulity as the succession of savage titles battered against his ears.

"Fierce lookin' fellows, ain't they? Seems like they'd just as soon tear a man to pieces as look at him. But you're welcome, all of you—welcome as a woman in a feather bed on a frosty night. Come right on inside." The arm carrying the fiddle made an all encompassing gesture. "I got a good fire goin', an' there's licker in the jug. We'll make a night of it this night; we'll set the brush afire an' howl the hoot owls right down outa the trees!"

It was an old house, a house of high ceilings and wide plank floors and half-furnished rooms, with a pile of eight-foot logs blazing on a hearth so wide it took up half a wall. There were great leather-covered chairs, the leather split and the horsehair and excelsior coming out through the gaps. Half a dozen family portraits hung askew on whitewashed plaster walls. Brown-smoked hams and strings of onions and cloth bags of peppers and herbs and spices swayed from the ceiling. A long-barreled squirrel gun was slung over the mantle and a shotgun was cradled on two sets of deer horns over the door. They caught the smell of woodsmoke and roasting meats and home-cured tobacco.

Fiddley's liquor was mellow and inexhaustible. Dinner was a high-piled, overflowing feast, served by half a dozen Negro women who scurried back and forth between the table and the kitchen, white headdresses bobbing up and down, warm voices chortling with laughter.

The liquor and the food and the sight and sound of Fiddley had soothed Melissa into a catlike contentment. During and after a long dinner, her troubles seemed far away and she was warm and completely relaxed with no need plucking at her except a lazily sensuous desire to be caressed and petted. Her reservations in regard to Mallonee had drifted away on the tide of this new heartsease, and she knew that if he desired her tonight, she would yield herself without even a faint pretence of reluctance. She closed her eyes, drowsy in the heat of the fire, scarcely attentive to the men's conversation.

"How'd you like to hear some real good old hoedown music?" Fiddley proposed. "Most usually I play an' call th' sets when there's a square dance anywheres in th' district. If it happens you got a taste for fiddlin'—"

"I'd love to hear you play, Fiddley." Melissa's eyes met Mallonee's, and she had to restrain another fit of laughter. "Do play for us and call some sets while you're playing."

Fiddley's eyes sparkled as he picked up the fiddle and tucked it under his chin. He perched himself on the extreme edge of a straight-backed chair, and he lifted his head and half-closed his eyes as the bow swept down over the strings.

"All join hands and circle right." His voice boomed and roared above the breathless quick-step of the fiddle. "Meet your honey and hold her tight—circle eight till you all get straight—swing yore gal like swingin' on a gate...."

It was almost midnight, and the music was over and the lights were out and Melissa and Mallonee were in a vast room with an immense four-poster that had a red quilted comforter and the clean smell of freshly laundered linen about it. Mallonee and Melissa faced each other, still amused at the recollections of Fiddley Flanders they'd been accumulating through the evening.

Melissa's smile faded as she looked into Mallonee's eyes. "Darling—" she whispered.

"Sure?" he asked her.

"Sure I'm sure," she said, and his arms reached out and closed around her.

CHAPTER SEVEN

SPIKED-NAILED FINGERS OF FEAR had been clawing at Dorsey Wilcox since the moment he'd read Charlotte's note—four days ago, now. It wasn't that he was a coward, he told himself; a man who'd come so far and so fast in the world couldn't be a coward. But when it came right down to the showdown he never could stand up to men like Dale Mallonee and Jeff McCutcheon.

He slammed the roll-top desk shut and got up and reached for his hat. There wasn't any use trying to get any work done while his mind was whirling and jumping like a squirrel in a cage. Loosh Maggard—Wilcox had taken him off his job of deputy sheriff and made him his personal bodyguard as soon as he got Charlotte's letter—had been loafing next to the upstairs window of Wilcox's office with his booted feet hoisted high on the office table. He let his feet slam down to the floor and cocked his head to one side to look up at Wilcox, his disreputable black slouch hat tipped down over his hard eyes.

"Goin' to stir some, boss?"

His voice said that he didn't really give a damn and that he was even faintly contemptuous of any man who had to have a bodyguard because he couldn't take care of himself. He's a hard-handed, cocksure sort of a bastard, Wilcox decided with a flare of resentment, but I've got to put up with him. I'll use him while I need him and if he ever tries to hold it over me later on, I'll arrange for him to have an accident.

"I'm going down to the hotel and have a drink," Wilcox said aloud. "It's just about time for the stage from Rolla to come in, and I'm looking for some land deeds that ought to be on it. Get up on your feet and let's go. Chances are I'll break down and buy you a drink, too."

Maggard grinned and got up and settled his gunbelt around his hips as he followed Wilcox to the door. Arch Ritland was squatting on his heels on the board sidewalk at the foot of the stairs. Wilcox had added him to his private army the same day he'd added Loosh. The same duties, the same obligation, except that Arch was supposed to stay far enough away from Loosh so that they wouldn't both be gunned down in a single blast. He grunted as they went past him, and when they were thirty feet down the street, he got to his feet and went slouching after them. They went straight across the square, their boots sloshing in the mud as they ducked around the farm wagons and the teams that were tied to the wooden hitch rail around the courthouse.

The square was no busier than it usually was on a Thursday morning when court was not in session. Two young clerks, white aprons tied around their waists and embroidered elastic armbands holding up their shirt sleeves, were hanging up sets of harness and blue Kentucky jeans and men's boots and plow points on a row of pegs across the front of Beardon's General Store, where they'd attract the trade of the passers-by. A hand-lettered sign tacked up over the door said: "We Take Flour, Meal, Bacon, Linsey and All Kinds of Country Produce in Trade."

Sam Williamson had fifteen or twenty Negroes, male and female, manacled together with an ankle chain, and was urging them across the road toward a raised platform where he held his slave auctions on Thursdays. Measuring them as a man might measure horseflesh in which he had no particular interest, Wilcox decided that few if any of them would be any good. Castoffs, he thought, from some of the hill farms down to the south, maybe; or field hands that some family emigrating west had been obliged to sell in order to get money enough to push on with.

The town women were bustling in and out of the stores, intent and absorbed in their weekly orgy of buying the provisions and supplies their households would need. They were soberly dressed in long calico dresses, with the new Philadelphia flower bonnets on their heads—except those few who still clung to the stiffly starched, and widewinged sunbonnets. The well-to-do ones were trailed by white-shawled Negro women wearing bandannas, each slave with a basket on her arm to carry home whatever items her mistress decided to buy.

The lean-shanked clodbusters from the ridges were standing at the edge of the sidewalks, talking in slow voices and spitting amber streams of tobacco juice into the muddy street. They were lanky, rough, whiskered men in homemade hickory shirts and wide-brimmed black hats, their linsey-woolsey pants stuffed into homemade cowhide boots caked with mud and manure. Some of them spoke as Wilcox went by, and he waved, stopping to pass the time of day with a few of them. In his role of moneylender and banker, he'd acquired mortgages on more than one of their rocky, isolated farms, almost lost down in the hills. It was smart to keep on the good side of them. Sooner or later they'd send their brothers and their cousins in to see him when times were hard and a man was willing to pay the ruinous twenty per cent interest that he charged.

The hotel was half a block off the square on St. Louis Street, with the barroom opening directly off the lobby. He didn't go through the lobby, for it was possible that Jean might be there, and he didn't want to talk to her that morning. She was pushing him to quit Charlotte and marry her, and they'd had words about it up in her room at the hotel the night before. But he wasn't going to get Charlotte against him now. Not until he'd cleared up this trouble with Mallonee. If he was fool enough to do that, she'd team up with Mallonee quicker than you could wink your eyes, and between the two of them...

Arch took a chair at one of the tables, tilting it back against the wall and hooking his heels into its rungs as Wilcox and Loosh went on to the bar, waving and speaking to the crowd already there as they crossed the room. Old Colonel Kilpatrick—who was a colonel by courtesy only—was erect and square-shouldered behind the bar. He moved down to meet them, offering them a good morning in the courtly, faintly superior manner that he affected. Almost seventy, he stood as straight as an arrow and claimed to have trapped beaver in the Rockies with Kit Carson and Jim Bridger years before. His hair was as white as snow, and he wore it long, sweeping the tops of his shoulders.

"Why, Colonel—" Wilcox had learned to make his voice hearty and jovial when other men were watching him—"I think we'll have a little of that special Kentucky bourbon of yours, and we'd be mighty honored if you'd join us in a taste of it this morning."

"Why, thank you, Dorsey. I believe I will take one with you, since you're kind enough to offer it."

He set out a bottle and three glasses and when they were filled, he lifted his and said, "Your very good health, Dorsey, and yours, Loosh." They tossed the drinks down and Wilcox felt his nerves relax a little. The whisky was warm and comforting inside him, blunting his fear. He slapped his glass down on the bar with an assurance he hadn't had before, and looked around the room to see if there was anyone there who'd repay the effort of initiating and maintaining a conversation with them.

A horn sounded twice, far up St. Louis Street to the east, and a teen-aged boy outside the saloon began to yell in a voice that changed ludicrously from a thundering bass to a piping treble. Wilcox tossed the paper aside and followed the crowd that was pushing its way out through the doorway to watch the Rolla stage come in. Loosh was at his heels, and when they reached the sidewalk, he saw that Arch had gone around through the hotel lobby and come out into the street some thirty feet away, where he could keep an eye on both of them.

The stage swung around the shallow bend that edged Judge Prentiss's mansion and came roaring down the middle of the rutted road. The guard balanced his shotgun across his knees with one hand while he blew an ear-splitting volley of blasts on his hand horn. The driver whooped as he jerked his horses back on their heels, and the stage slid to a stop directly in front of the crowd gathered on the uneven sidewalk.

"Fastest damn stage line anywhere in the West, boys!" he howled. "Four minutes ahead of time, an' we'll roll again quick as we get some fresh horses." He leaned down and back toward the door of the stage. "You've come to Springfield, Missouree-ee, folks. If you've a mind to light here you want to jump spry. We ain't goin' to be here no longer than it takes to hitch up an' git!"

The door swung open and the crowd on the sidewalk pushed up a little closer to see who was going to get out. A man came first, a pudgy St. Louis drummer in a checked suit and a derby hat, with a heavy gold watch chain across his brocaded vest. He turned and held out his hand and a woman appeared in the doorway, a vividly handsome, black-haired woman who took the drummer's hand and stepped down out of the coach, lifting her blue woolen skirt and the peeping lace-edged petticoats she wore up out of the mud with a slim, elegantly gloved hand. She looked around, a half-smile twitching at the corners of her lips.

"I'm Mrs. Melissa McCutcheon," she announced. Her voice was like clear water and bright sunshine and a south wind blowing low through the trees. "I'm looking for my husband—Jeffrey McCutcheon."

Her look ranged questioningly along the row of gaping faces, but her eyes stopped and steadied when they came to Wilcox, almost as if she had recognized him and singled him out for her questions.

"Can't—can't any of you tell me where to find him?" It seemed to Wilcox that she was appealing directly to him, forgetting and dismissing the others around her. "It's been a long trip from Kentucky, and I'm very eager to see him."

The staring faces seemed to be wrapped in silence. Out of them all, there weren't half a dozen men who didn't know that Jeffrey McCutcheon had disappeared a month ago, and that his disappearance was linked with the death of the immigrant who'd had his throat cut one night in Tiff's Wagon Yard. Wilcox stared at her, hostile-eyed, but still feeling his blood beat faster when he looked at her. A handsome woman—why, damn it, she was one of the handsomest women he'd ever clapped eyes on—but she was still the Melissa McCutcheon that Charlotte had warned him about. But what was she doing coming in on a stage from the east when a week ago she'd been riding up from the south with Mallonee and his Indians? He shook his head, confused, feeling doubt and fear crawling in him again. But his life depended upon what he could find out from her. He forced a smile and stepped forward, sketching a bow and sweeping off his hat in the same gesture.

"Mrs. McCutcheon," he said soothingly, "it just happens Jeff's out of town right now. I'm Dorsey Wilcox, an old friend of his. I'll be proud if you'll let me help you any way that I can."

"Why—why, that's kind of you, Mr. Wilcox!" She smiled at him, and her teeth were white and even and her lower lip was very full and red. He felt a sharp stinging racing through his body, the same sense of wanting and demanding he'd known the first time he ever saw Charlotte naked and fair-skinned and touched with moonlight back in Mississippi.

"Do you know when Jeffrey will be back, Mr. Wilcox?"

"No," he admitted, "I don't know just exactly, but if you'll let me, I'll be glad to help you find lodgings where you'll be comfortable until he does come in."

She had a devil in her, he could see that in the tilt of her head and the veiled invitation in the demure look that was not really demure at all.

"Why, yes," she agreed. "I will have to find some place to stay, won't I? A place that's comfortable and clean and has a—" the deviltry in her eyes flared up a little—"and has a little privacy about it."

She put her hand in the curve of his arm, and it seemed to him that the formal gesture had suddenly established the sharp, intense intimacy between them that a man sometimes knows with a woman when whatever barriers there may have been between them go crashing down as abruptly as if they'd been swept away by a tidal wave. There in the open, with the crowd staring and the sharp March sunlight white and clear around them, he had the feeling that she was in his arms and that she belonged there and that it was right to have her there.

And then the fact of who she was and what she was came back like a dark wave. His nerves went tight and his mind snapped shut. Panic held him and he cursed himself for a fool who'd almost been gulled by the sight and the scent and the touch of the woman who had come here to destroy him. His mouth hardened.

"We'll take a look at the hotel first," he said curtly, and his voice was edged and bitter in spite of all he could do. "If it doesn't suit you, we'll try to find another place."

In the end, the other place was revealed as a neat, unoccupied little furnished four-room house just north of the square and of a tiny stream called Jordan's Branch. She'd looked at the hotel and wrinkled her nose and said something under her breath about Merigay's Tavern—and it had suited Wilcox as well when she'd rejected it. His own room was there and, directly adjacent to it, was the little two-room apartment he'd maintained all winter for Jean Bruillot. There'd have been danger, he thought, in letting Jean be too close to Melissa—Jean had a snug, compact little body that could set a man on fire, but she was French and there was a definite fire in her eyes that could change into a furious jealousy and violence in the space between two heartbeats.

The house Melissa finally chose was one that had belonged to an old German couple who'd died the winter before. Wilcox had bought it from their son in St. Louis, with a vague idea of moving Jean in there and giving up his own room at the hotel. But the Frenchwoman hadn't liked the idea of leaving the hotel. Too far from the square and too lonely, she'd said flatly, so he'd let it stand empty till he could decide what to do with it. It was filled with the heavy old handmade furniture the Gruenthers had brought with them from the old country, round woven carpets on the scrubbed pine floors, a row of decorated Bavarian beer mugs across the crowded mantel, and a wide four-poster feather bed topped with layer after layer of handmade eiderdown quilts.

"If you'll let me," he'd suggested as they were saying good-by in her doorway, "I'd like to drop by this evening and see if there's anything I can do to help you get settled." The physical attraction that wouldn't be denied had a hand in it, even though he told himself that his real purpose—his only purpose, damn it—was to find out what she could tell him about Mallonee.

Melissa took a step closer to him and laid her hand on his arm as she looked up at him, deep-eyed and serious, infusing the casual moment with the suggestion of a significant prelude between them.

"You've been wonderful to me." Her fingers tightened on his arm. "I can't tell you how much I appreciate it. And please believe that you're welcome here any time you want to come!" She smiled at him then, with her nose wrinkling and her eyes closing a little as if they shared some intimate and delicious secret between them. "It would be wonderful of you to come and see me tonight! I'll be—waiting for you."

He went out the door and across the porch with the implication of her words and the scent of her perfume weaving a sharp sense of excitement and anticipation in him. Loosh got up from his seat on the steps, and they started back up Boonville Road toward the square with Arch thirty paces behind them.

"You want me to bodyguard you against her?" Loosh said. He guffawed and slapped his thigh and jerked his black hat down a little tighter over one eye. "By God, Dorsey, I wouldn't charge you nothin' for lookin' after a piece like that—not even if it come to a point of rasslin' her to keep you outa harm's way!"

"I don't know," Wilcox said slowly. "I'm just not sure."

He didn't know. His mind, the hard, untouched core of it, reminded him that Melissa had been riding up from the south with Mallonee, and that Charlotte's note warned him against exactly the situation that he was in now. But it was hard to be sure. The way she'd warmed up to him there at the last, and the way her fingers had tightened on his arm just as he was leaving…

He'd taken women away from better men than Mallonee in the past, he told himself. It just might be—reason mocked the self-deception, but he clung to it stubbornly—it just might be that he was going to do it again.

CHAPTER EIGHT

T HE NIGHT WAS BLACK as the pits of hell and a raw wind was
cold and pitiless out of the north. There was no light anywhere
except the candle glow from Melissa's windows when Dorsey
Wilcox rapped on her door. Back by the road, Arch Ritland had
found such shelter as he could behind a leafless hedge row. Loosh
Maggard, bitterly profane, had turned the corner of the house
and found a corner between the chimney and the wall where the
wind could not reach him.

"You better make it short an' sweet, Dorsey," he'd growled
mutinously. "I promised you I'd try to keep you from gettin'
killed, but I sure as hell never set out to freeze myself to death
gettin' it done."

"You do your job and let me do mine." Dorsey's voice had
been edged and his hands had jerked at his belt, for the fear had
come back on him after he'd left Melissa—the fear of Mallonee,
the fear of death. His guts were tied into a hard knot as he waited
for her to answer his knock and a cold whispering inside of him
kept telling him that he had to make her tell him where Mallonee
was and what he was planning to do. He had to know. He had to
find out before Mallonee killed him.

The door swung open, and he saw her smiling and holding
out her hand to him, slim and sweetly soft and glowing like ivory
and ebony and gold with the yellow candlelight behind her. He
caught the scent of her perfume as he stepped forward and for an
instant they were so close together that he could see the delicately
soft texture of her skin and almost feel the warmth of her breath

against his cheek. His breath hung in his throat as his whole body tightened in sudden expectation.

His hands came up, eager, but Melissa had stepped back, half turned toward the room in a posture of invitation and still smiling at him so that he could not be sure whether she had moved deftly out of his reach or whether she simply had not seen the beginning, and so missed the significance, of the gesture he had begun.

"It's so lovely to see you!"

There was a warm breathlessness in her voice, an excitement as revealing and as proudly, as frankly desirous as if she had stripped herself before him. Her eyes clung to him, hinting at a thousand things she had not said.

"You must be so cold." Her fingertips touched his hand, and then suddenly her palm was tight against his and her fingers had curled themselves around his wrist. "Let's go over to the fire. Wouldn't you like that?" She moved a little, pulling him gently toward the intimacy of the fire blazing upon the hearth. A log crumbled and the flames flared high, the light suddenly fierce and brilliant behind her, striking through the sheer scarlet of her dress so that for an instant all the sweet loveliness of her figure was revealed in silhouette.

"Wouldn't you like that?" she asked again, and her eyes touched the love seat that had been drawn up to face the fire. "We could sit down there and—and talk—while you get warm again."

"I'd like that—yes."

His nervousness and his fear had slipped away, and he was suddenly sure of himself; sure of himself and sure of her, lustful and self-confident and even a little contemptuous because this conquest had been so easy. He'd take her—the thought of it was savage in his mind—and in the taking he'd wring her dry of every drop of information she could give him of Mallonee and his plans. He slipped his arm around her waist as they sat down, and she sighed and let her body go soft in the circle of his arm.

"You've been awfully good to me today." Her voice had the purr in it of a contented kitten. "And it's so wonderful of you because I know you've so many important things to do." Her hand slipped out and covered his, silk-soft, fire-warmed. "One of the men on the stage told me about you. He was so envious of you, of your mill and your farms and your bank and all the wonderful success you've had here."

He felt his body tremble with secret laughter. Damned if you got all that from any man on a stage, he thought derisively. Mallonee told you that, and Mallonee told you what to say and you're saying it very nicely—but you don't know that I know Mallonee sent you here.

"I've been lucky here," he forced a note of false humility into his voice. "But I was damn lucky to have enough to get a start here at all."

"Lucky? But I thought—" She checked herself. "I don't understand what you mean."

And why not tell her, he thought? Tell Melissa a part of it and tell it my way, and tear down her precious Mallonee for her.

"It was back in Mississippi." His arm tightened around her, his fingers cupping the curve of her breast as he caught her mood of acquiescence in the little snuggling movement against him and the half sigh on her lips. "I was in the cotton factoring trade down there, and I had a good business. But I had a bad partner, too, and he almost ruined me."

"Oh, no! How did he do that?"

"Oh, the regular way. His name was Mallonee, and he was a good-looking devil. Smart enough, too, on most things—but he couldn't let the women alone. Couldn't be around a pretty woman without moving heaven and earth to get into bed with her, and it didn't make any difference which one of them it was. One of them was as good as another as far as he was concerned."

"And you say that was—Mallonee?"

"Yes, that was his name. Dale Mallonee. He was part Cherokee Indian, and he wanted to live like one, too. Spent all his own money on whisky and women, and when that was gone he began to spend the company money. He'd done a pretty good job of getting away with a lot of it before I found out what he was doing and broke up our partnership."

"Then—then *you* broke up the partnership. Oh, I didn't know it was like that—"

"Why, no, you couldn't have known. Not unless you knew Mallonee—" He let the suggestion hang between them in the air, but she only shook her head and tightened her fingers around his hand. "That's about all there is to it, actually. He took it pretty hard when I kicked him out. Swore he'd hunt me down and get even and all the rest of it—but he'd been drunk for a month and he was drunk the last time I saw him, and you can't pay too much attention to what a barrelhouse booze fighter has to say."

"Oh, but if he's like you say he is—aren't you afraid he will find you and try to—to do something terrible to you?"

"He won't hurt me too much as long as I've got two bodyguards with me night and day." Tell him that, he thought, and let him think about how fast he'd get killed if he tried to walk in on me. "But I'd want to know it if he was in this part of the country." He leaned forward so that his face was against her cheek, his voice low and intimate and unmistakably suggestive. "I'd be mighty grateful to anyone who tipped me off about that. Mighty grateful, and you know I've got the power around here to make things mighty easy and pleasant for somebody if I wanted to do it."

"I know. Yes—I know that."

Melissa's fingers moved a little along the back of his hand, up his wrist, and he saw that she was biting her lip and staring into the fire with a frown gathering between her eyes. I've got her on the run now, he thought triumphantly. She's begun to worry about her precious Mallonee and about his other women and about whether he's lied to her or not. She's wondering if she wouldn't be smart to change sides while she still can.

"If Mallonee came riding into Springfield now—" he made his voice even and relentless, driving home the spike of final fear— "he wouldn't live long enough to get across the square, no matter how many men he had with him. This is my town. I can make it damned rough or I can make it damned smooth for anybody here—depending on whether they want to play it my way or some other way. You understand what I mean, Mrs. McCutcheon? You understand just exactly what I mean?"

"Oh, yes—yes. I didn't before, but I do now. Oh, darling, believe me. I do understand now."

"Then maybe you can tell me something about Mallonee. Maybe you—" his voice roughened into a sneering taunt— "maybe that man you were talking to on the stage told you something about Mallonee that I'd like to know. Something about like where he is and what he's figuring on doing next and when he's figuring on doing it. Maybe you'd know something about that, wouldn't you?"

He felt Melissa's body shiver and then stiffen against him, and it seemed to him that he caught a hint of desperation in her eyes.

"Oh, please don't ask me that. Please don't ask me that now. I've got to think about all this—I don't know, darling."

"By hell, if you do know—" His hand jerked free from her fingers, darted forward, clamped down on her shoulder as he spun her around to face him. "You'll tell me, or I'll make you wish—"

Her hands fluttered up to touch his face, and he saw that her lips were trembling and there were sudden tears in her eyes.

"Oh, please, darling, give me just a little time. It won't make any difference. It won't bring any harm to you, I swear it won't!"

She pulled herself tight against him and her lips were suddenly hot and wet and very sweet against his mouth. He tried to harden himself against her, to hold and retain the dark ruthlessness that had driven him, but he could feel it slipping away, smothered and softened and dissolved into desire beneath the shattering feel of her body and her lips.

"But if I knew—" He tried to shake himself free from the spell that she was weaving around him. "If I knew now—"

"Not now, darling," her lips were whispering against his, her body suddenly urgent and demanding, kindling dark traceries of fire that blotted out his determination, his instinct of vigilance, against her. Maybe a little later then.

"All right, then," he said roughly. His hands tore at her bodice, pulling it apart, finding the sharp curves of her breasts, the hard-pointed tips of them. The breath was stabbing through his lungs and his eyes were like an animal's. "We'll go your way now, then, and after that—"

For an instant Melissa surrendered to him utterly, her body writhing against him and little cries of eagerness on her lips. Then, suddenly, she was out of his arms and on her feet, just beyond his reach, one hand twisting the edges of her torn bodice together and tragedy in her eyes.

The move had come so suddenly that it left him staring and bewildered. Graceless and empty-armed, baffled and undone in this sudden anti-climax, he could only gape at her, too amazed to try to call her back, too stunned and confounded to blaze into raging fury.

"What the hell's gone wrong with you—"

"Oh, darling, I'm so sorry—but I can't. Not with those men peering in through the window."

"Those men? Loosh, you mean? Loosh and Arch—my bodyguards? Hell, they're not peeking in through any windows! They're not—"

"But they know you're here, darling. And they're just outside and I just can't."

"Well, by hell, I never ran into this before! I've got a damn good notion to strip you and—"

But the fire and the strength had gone out of him, and it was all bluff and bravado now. With the abject helplessness of a weak man, a man who had known too long that his brassy shell of dominance was a shell and nothing more, he had accepted this defeat—or this deferment—as he had long since learned to accept the endless chronicle of the defeats and deferments that his own weakness had brought upon him. He got to his feet and stood staring down at her, anger fighting inside him against desire now, the furious, almost feminine vindictiveness of the weakling against the self-abasement of the fool.

"Hell," he said helplessly. "I can't send them away. You know that. Not with Mallonee—"

"Oh, darling—" Her voice was suddenly tender, compassionate— "you've nothing to fear from Mallonee. Not now—not since I know how things really are and—and since I know you. But you can't send them away now. It's too late for that tonight—but there's tomorrow night."

She took two quick steps forward so that there was no more than the width of a man's hand between them. Her hands touched his chest.

"I want you so, darling!" Her voice was a husky whisper, shaken with passion, promising many things. "Can't you come back to me tomorrow night—without them? We can be alone, just the two of us together."

A last faint measure of common sense struggled to assert itself inside his mind.

"But suppose I did come without them? Suppose Mallonee—"

"Mallonee won't come to Springfield, darling. Mallonee won't ever bother you again. I can tell you that much now, and I'll tell you the rest of it tomorrow night—if you come alone."

"I can count on that, then? If I come alone? If I don't bring them with me?"

"Oh, you know you can!"

The door closed behind him, and after a moment Melissa turned and went back to the love seat before the fire. She dropped down on it and let her hands drop into her lap as if she were exhausted. A door opened and closed softly at the back of the house and she sat without moving while the minutes ticked by. Finally Tahchee came into the room on silent feet.

"They're gone? You're sure that they're gone?" She lifted her head to look at him, and he saw that there were dark circles below her eyes.

"Gone," he agreed. "Gone across the little river. Gone into town."

"Thank God," she said wearily. "Thank God for that. You heard it all, Tahchee?"

He nodded grimly. His fingers touched the knife thrust into his belt and he frowned toward the closed door as if he regretted the opportunity that had passed.

"I heard," he agreed. "Now I tell Mallonee."

"Tell him he must be here tomorrow night. Tell him Wilcox will be here without his guards. And Tahchee—" She hesitated and her hand went up to her throat. "Tell him I love him and I need him very much."

CHAPTER NINE

MELISSA WOKE UP THE NEXT MORNING in her great wide bed with the eiderdown quilt upon it. The cottage was cold and the March wind was moaning beneath the eaves of the house—and she was afraid. She turned her head to look out through the small-paned window of the bedroom and saw that the day was as gray and luckless as her own spirit. There was no sun, no light, no brightness, and the sky was sullen with a grisly army of murky, low-hanging clouds massed across it.

It had been very bad the night before, when Wilcox was there. Thinking of it, she felt as if she was stained with dirt and dishonor that she could never wash off again. It was all very well to tell herself that there had been no other way, she had never played that game with a man before and the remembrance of it was bitter as gall.

She had been safe enough—she'd been more than safe, with Tahchee hidden in the bedroom and his hand plucking hungrily at his knife all the time Wilcox was lying to her and playing the fool and trying to seduce or browbeat her. If Wilcox had known of that—and of Tahchee's fanatic loyalty to Mallonee and his stoic acceptance of the fact that now she belonged to Mallonee and so must be protected at any cost—the man would be halfway to the Missouri River by now instead of planning another visit tonight.

And there were things that had to be done before that visit. When they'd planned this thing, she and Mallonee, they'd known that there'd be nothing he could do with Wilcox inside the town of Springfield—nothing except kill him outright, and there'd be little to be gained by that. No, the plan was to kidnap him and get him away and then let him ransom himself, if he could, by signing over enough of his property to Mallonee to replace the money he'd stolen.

But to do that they'd have to know what property he had. Without that, he'd dupe them and in the end it would all come to nothing. And that was what she had to do today. She had to find Wilcox's office and make her way into it and hunt through his records there until she found some description of what he had. It was risky, knowing as little of his habits or the habits of the town as she did, but there was no way to delay it, for Mallonee and the Cherokees would be there, and it had to be done before that.

Melissa tossed the quilt aside and slipped on a warm dressing gown and belted it tight around her waist. The fireplace in the living room seemed gray and lifeless at first, but she poked in the ashes and turned over the unburnt ends of last night's logs until a pocket of orange-yellow coals appeared. She fed first small sticks and then larger ones to them until the flames began to leap up and the draft roared in the chimney and the heat was so strong that she had to step back to the edge of the hearth.

By the time she'd made coffee and had a cup of it in front of the fire, she had begun to think more of Mallonee and the future and less of Wilcox and Jeff and the past, so that the world was brighter than it had been half an hour before. The question of Jeffrey still hung in the air—but it was a question she knew how to answer now. He was her husband—or had been *true enough*—but he'd run away and left her and since then he'd murdered and killed and robbed and become the hired bravo of such a scoundrel as Wilcox. Whatever debt she may have owed him in the beginning was washed out now.

It was a little past noon when she came out of her door and turned south toward the little stream Wilcox had called Jordan's Branch, and neared the town square of Springfield. It was a busy place, farm wagons drawn by straining horses or by double-yoked teams of oxen creaked past her up the hill, bound for the square of false-fronted wooden stores and peeled-pole hitching racks and plank sidewalks that made up the center of the town. There was a two-story courthouse in the middle of the square and streets ran out from it in four directions. There was no lack of people upon the streets, young and old, white and black, rustics in cowhide boots and gentlemen in tailored broadcloth and starched, immaculate linen.

A handsome young woman in a black varnished carriage with shining red wheels relaxed against its cushions while the white-aproned merchant who'd come out into the mud of the street to take her order bowed and scraped before her and her Negro coachmen gentled the matched bay mares that drew the carriage. Not twenty feet away a hill family in a two-wheeled cart drawn by a single ox stared goggle-eyed at the sights and wonders about them, the father perched on the edge of the cart with a holstered pistol at his hip and a bull whip in his hand, the woman's face drawn and lined and as timid as a rabbit's as she peered out between the wings of her faded sunbonnet.

Melissa had put on a plain black dress with a dark blue jacket and a simple poke bonnet, so that she might be as inconspicuous as possible. In so small and isolated a town she knew she would already have become a target for speculation and gossip. The fact that she was looking for a runaway husband, that the wealthiest man in town, Dorsey Wilcox, had immediately become her escort, and that he had called at her cottage the night before—oh, yes, the tongues would be wagging fast enough, and there'd be plenty of sharp eyes and busy tongues to see what she did and report on it. And yet she had to find Dorsey Wilcox's office, and find it when he was not in it.

She was halfway along the south side of the square, and still with no clear idea of what she was to do next, when a mouse-haired, undersized young stripling in a white clerk's apron came stumbling out of a store doorway on to the sidewalk with his arms piled high with bundles that he was carrying to some farm wagon hitched at the sidewalk. It was too big a load for one youngster, and he was wavering even before the wind caught his wide apron and slapped it up over his face and sent him blundering into her before she could step aside and evade him.

For an instant they clung together like awkward dancers, the load in his arms swaying precariously as he tried to regain his balance and she tried to skip aside out of his way—and then the topmost sack toppled forward and another followed it. As he tried frantically to twist and save them, she was flung back against the wall of the building and the boy went sprawling on the ground at her feet. Her bonnet was pushed down over her face and her skirts flew everywhere. All up and down the street men and women had turned to stare at them and guffaw, and half a dozen turned and started toward them. Flat on his rump on the sidewalk, long legs stretched straight out in front of him, the boy was pushing himself up to a sitting position and staring up at her out of a wide-eyed face that was horrified and abject.

"Lord God, ma'am—" His face flushed red as fire and he slapped one hand over his mouth. "Beggin' your pardon, ma'am, but I never meant to do nothin' like this. I couldn't see which way I was goin', an' then when th' wind hit me—"

She'd had an impulse to give him a tongue-lashing that would have raised blisters, but she couldn't snap out at this young hobbledehoy with the shame in his eyes any more than she could have taken a whip to a young colt who'd blundered into a pasture fence and hurt himself.

"It's all right," she said shakily. Most of the breath had been knocked out of her and she was having trouble jerking her bonnet back into place against the wind; but neither of those things was as important as her need to get out of sight and out of the public eye before too many people—especially Dorsey Wilcox—saw her and began to wonder about her. She sent a quick look over her shoulder and it seemed to her that the store he'd come out of was empty. "You're keeping store by yourself?" she demanded.

"I am right now, ma'am." He had scrambled to his feet and was trying to gather up his load again. "Pa's went home to dinner an' th' clerk's drunk today an' didn't show up. There ain't nobody here but me right now. I'll be happy to try to wait on you, though, if I can make out to do it."

"Maybe you can," she said. "Let's go inside and see." It was a quick decision, too quick perhaps, but the half-dozen men who'd started toward them weren't more than twenty feet away, and she had to get away before they began to ask questions. "Have you got all your bundles? Bring them back inside then. You can take them out again later."

Melissa held the door open for him, and he stumbled through it. She followed him and slammed the door hard behind her. The men on the sidewalk stopped and stared as if they half suspected that it had been slammed in their faces, and then they began to talk and laugh and gradually drift away. It was dark and gloomy inside the store, but that was what she wanted. The boy put his bundles down and wiped his hands on his apron and turned back to her with a tentative, shy smile.

"I'm right pleased you didn't take no offense, ma'am," he said awkwardly. "An' now if you'll tell me how, so I can serve you, I'll be proud to get at it."

"I'm looking for Mr. Wilcox's office," she said hurriedly. "Dorsey Wilcox. You know him, don't you?"

"Ain't nobody in Springfield don't know Mr. Wilcox, but he ain't in his office right now. It's jest right up over th' store here. I seen him an' Loosh Maggard come down the stairs an' go to the hotel fifteen or twenty minutes ago. He ain't likely to be back for half an hour or more. Would you want me to send after him for you?"

"Oh, no! No—I don't want you to do that." It was a marvelous streak of luck, almost too good to be true. But the boy had said Wilcox would be back in half an hour. There was no time to lose. "You said you saw him come down the stairs—out in front you mean? Stairs that come out on the sidewalk?"

"Why, yes, ma'am. Right next to where you was standin' when I run over you. I can show you where they are."

He started toward the front door, but Melissa motioned him back while she tried to collect her thoughts. Heaven only knew how many people had seen the collision on the sidewalk and might be watching from the corners of their eyes to see her come out of the store. If they saw her going up the stairs to Dorsey Wilcox's office, it would be only a matter of minutes till he'd be told about it and come hurrying across the square after her. There had to be another way.

"Aren't there any back stairs?" she demandad. "Any that go up from the back of the building?"

The youngster stared at her as if he thought she had taken leave of her senses.

"Wouldn't be no use in a man buildin' back stairs to a buildin' when the ones out to front was solid—" he began, but she waved his protest into silence.

Melissa studied him, and the guilelessness and obvious desire to make amends that she saw reassured her. She had to have help, and in order to get it she had to reveal a little to someone—and this boy was likely to be as safe a confidant as she could have found if she'd searched the streets of Springfield from morning till night.

"What's your name?" she said.

"Why, I'm Andy Parkinson, ma'am. My pa owns this store. I work on the farm mostly, when I ain't obliged to pitch in an' help him around here."

"All right, Andy." She took a quick step forward and laid her hand on his arm. "I'm going to tell you a secret, and I'm going to let you help me a little—if you will, and if you want to make up for running into me on the sidewalk out there."

"Land, ma'am—" the red deepened in his face— "I'll be proud to do whatever I can do to make up for that. You just tell me what it is you want."

"I want to get up to Dorsey Wilcox's office without anyone seeing me go up there. And I don't want anyone to go and tell Mr. Wilcox that I'm there or that I've been there. Do you understand that, Andy?"

"Well, now—" He brought up one hand and rubbed his chin doubtfully. "I can't rightly say that I understand too much about it, but if that's what you want I'll do whatever I can to help. But what I don't see is how you're goin' to get up there less you walk up them stairs."

"How about a ladder? This building's got windows in the back of it—it must have. Haven't you got a ladder around here that would reach those windows?"

"Why, sure," he agreed, but the doubt was growing in his face. "Got an old patched-up thing out there I used when I was paintin' last fall. But you ain't figurin' on skinnin' up no ladder to get to Wilcox's office, are you? A lady, all dressed up fine like you be?"

"Never mind about how I'm dressed," she assured him. She tightened her fingers on his arm and he looked up at her inquiringly. "You just get the ladder and put it up there. You'll do that for me, won't you, Andy?"

He took a deep breath and his head came up as if he had just received an accolade of knighthood.

"You're mighty right I will," he said firmly. "You want to get at it right now?"

"Right now," Melissa said, and he nodded and turned away toward the back of the store. She hurried after him.

The window the ladder touched was unlocked. Melissa hammered and tugged and pushed against its dried-paint immobility until it came open, while Andy steadied the ladder beneath her until she managed to crawl inside the window.

She was in a narrow hallway that had two doors opening off it on either side. At its far end she could see the banisters and the landing of the stairway that led down to the front of the building. Andy had told her that Wilcox occupied the two rooms on the east. "Uses th' front one for his office an' stacks up his old letters an' ledgers an' such in the other one," he'd said. A lawyer and a doctor, respectively, rented the two offices on the left, but the lawyer was riding circuit and the doctor had ridden off on a call. So she had the place to herself—until Wilcox and Loosh came back from the hotel.

Melissa had lost a good ten minutes talking in the store and finding the doubtful and decrepit ladder and getting it up against the back of the building, so that the half-hour Andy had mentioned had already shrunk to a bare twenty minutes. She ran down the hall and jerked open the door of Wilcox's office and slipped inside—and then she gasped and felt her heart sink inside her, for the place was a rat's nest of papers and ledgers and string-tied bundles of notes or mortgages and discarded newspapers and a thousand derelict items of business, without even a pretence of order or organization. It would have taken days to comb through it—and she had twenty minutes, or perhaps less. She took a deep breath and went across the room to the roll-top desk and began to go through the papers on top of it.

She knew nothing about business, and the clutter she found was all mystery and confusion. Invoices and receipts and bills of lading and canceled checks—she turned them all over, pawing at them like a dog digging out a mole, while her nerves stretched tighter and tighter with the realization that her own ignorance could very easily lead her to discard and throw aside the very thing that she was trying to find.

The pigeonholes were stuffed with more papers, and Melissa dragged them out and went through them with shaking fingers, the dust and dirt that had accumulated on them griming her hands and her dress, puffing up in clouds when she tried to blow it away, clinging to her like soot when she tried to brush it free. And it was all the same—an insoluble confusion.

She was breathing like a runner at the end of a hard race now, her fingers flying and her brain in a whirl. The minutes were ticking by and she knew no more about what Dorsey Wilcox owned and didn't own than she'd known when she first stepped into his office. Up in the courthouse tower a clock chimed once and she knew her half-hour was gone. She was ready to turn and run, when she plunged her hand into the last pigeonhole and came out with an envelope with a rubber band around it. It wasn't as dirty and dusty as the others had been, and when she turned it over she saw that someone had written across the face of it: "Tax statements, all properties."

For a moment Melissa stood motionless, trembling, almost afraid to open it, and then she ripped off the rubber band and jerked out the bundle of folded papers inside it and spread them open on top of the desk. The form of them was strange to her, but the meaning was clear enough. There were almost two dozen of them, each on a form from the county collector's office, each listing some piece of property that Dorsey Wilcox owned, each giving the description and valuation of that property and the amount of taxes assessed against it. As if to make it even more certain for her, someone, probably Wilcox himself, had identified the legal descriptions with an explanatory note scrawled on each one, so that the first she saw was identified as "Sawmill," the second as "Bank building," the next as "Findley River farm," and so on through the entire list.

This was what she'd prayed for, and what Mallonee needed to force Wilcox to make reparation to him! It seemed impossible that she had found it in the snarled confusion of such disorder, but she had it! And now her task was to get away with it. For a moment she considered walking boldly down the stairs and out into the street, but the risk of meeting Dorsey was too great. No, it would have to be the ladder again, and this time with no Andy to steady it for her, for she knew he'd gone back to the store as soon as he saw her safely inside.

Melissa glanced at the ruffled papers on the desk and it seemed to her that they were no more disordered than before. She pushed the long envelope down into the bodice of her dress and turned toward the door. She had just put her hand on the knob and started to jerk it open when she heard the sound of men's voices and their boot heels pounding on the stairway outside. She pulled the door open the merest crack and peered through it, her heart pounding and her breath caught tight in her lungs.

Dorsey Wilcox's head was just emerging above the head of the stairs and the man he'd called Loosh was two steps behind him. Half a dozen steps would bring them to the door of the office!

Melissa closed the door leading into the adjoining room. She fumbled at the knob, felt it turn, felt the door bind and hang. She threw her weight against it, felt it give and plunged through it into the black hole of the storeroom. She turned and pushed the door almost closed—she was afraid to try to force it shut for fear of the noise—and through the open crack she saw Wilcox and Loosh come sauntering into the office that she had just escaped.

Wilcox was smoking a cigar and Loosh was picking his teeth with the blade of an open pocket knife and belching gustily as his tribute to the meal they had just enjoyed at the hotel. Wilcox went across the room to his desk, and Melissa caught a breath of relief as she saw him sweep a mass of the papers aside with one arm before he dropped down into his chair and elevated his boots to the place the papers had occupied. He wouldn't know that they'd been disturbed, after he had scrambled them into a new and fantastic confusion himself. And Loosh obviously had no interest in either desk or papers, for he crossed the room to a chair beside a window and settled himself in it and scratched his ribs and fumbled through his pockets for a cigar that was the mate to Wilcox's, and then got it afire.

"So you won't be wantin' me or Arch with you tonight then, Dorsey." There was a touch of ridicule in Loosh's voice. "Leastwise, you told that black-haired gal of McCutcheon's that, an' made her believe you, didn't you?"

"I'm damned if I know whether she believed me or not. She acted like she did. But she's a damn fool, and she must think I'm one if she believes I'd call you off the job just because she asked me to. Hell's fire, she's Mallonee's woman, isn't she? Jeff had Charlotte write me a note and tell me that, didn't he? And she knows damn well that I know it, too, but I'll bet a horse against a hand axe she didn't know it when she came flouncing down off that stage."

Melissa caught her breath. He would have his guards with him tonight, then! And he did know about her association with Mallonee—although there hadn't been much doubt of that after his questions the night before. But that Jeff should have been the one to betray her to him! The shock of that turned her numb and sick for a minute.

Loosh's voice was rumbling again, and she put her ear to the door to hear what was being said.

"Thing I can't make out, Dorsey, is whether you're playing up to her just because she's a purty thing or whether you got somethin' else in mind."

"You mind your own damned business on that, Loosh." Wilcox's boots had come down off the desk and he was staring at Loosh angrily. "You just do what I tell you and let me mind the rest of my affairs without trying to stick your damned nose into them. You understand that, Loosh?"

"Hell yes, I understand you!" Loosh's voice was suddenly peevish and at the same time, it seemed to her, more than a little placatory.

Wilcox stared at him without moving a muscle and then he relaxed and let himself slump back into his chair.

"All right, Loosh," he said casually. "No need for us to stir up trouble with each other." He took a deep breath and she saw his shoulders rise and fall. "God knows I've got too damn much trouble already. I've got this woman on my hands and Jean's raising blue hell about that, and God only knows what Charlotte's going to say when she hears the straight of it. Lord, Loosh! Let's have a drink! Bring that jug over and let me take a crack at it before I have to start out again."

She didn't move out of her dusty hiding place until she'd heard them take their drink and go out the door and slam it behind them and go stamping down the stairs. Even then she waited for a while before she ventured to look out into the empty office.

She had had enough—too much for one day. And the awful night was still before her. She turned and ran down the hall to the back window and was half out of it before she saw the rickety ladder lying flat on the ground thirty feet below and realized that the gusty March wind had blown it down. It seemed to her then that she would collapse, but the thought of Wilcox's and Loosh's possible return drove her on. They hadn't said where they were going or when they would be back and the horror that was beginning to whirl in her brain admitted only one thought—escape.

Melissa turned and ran down the hall and plunged recklessly down the stairs, careless of who might or might not see her now, wanting nothing except to be free from this nightmare. She came out on to the sidewalk with a rush and almost collided with a red-headed woman who was just starting up the stairs. She was young and beautifully built and there was a foreign look about her.

The woman jerked back and stared at her, and for an instant she was too startled to do more than return the stare. Some instinct of concealment forced Melissa to try to smile at her and turn a phrase that would conceal where she had been.

"He isn't there," she said breathlessly. "The doctor, I mean—I was just up there and there's nobody in his office."

"The doctor!" The red-headed woman's voice was husky, smouldering almost. Her eyes seemed to pin Melissa to the wall. "But you're Jeffrey McCutcheon's wife—"

Melissa turned and ran toward Jordan's Branch and the cottage where she could catch her breath and collect her thoughts.

It seemed to her that she could feel the woman's eyes stabbing her in the back as she hurried away. And she could still hear the husky voice: "But you're Jeffrey McCutcheon's wife!"

CHAPTER TEN

CHARLOTTE SHERWOOD'S NERVES—she shook her head, reminding herself that when she'd come to Missouri with Dorsey she'd assumed the role of Charlotte Wilcox—were raw and quivering. She got up from the sofa and poked at the fire until it blazed brightly. Through the windows on either side of the fireplace she could see bare-limbed trees whipping in the wind and catch a glimpse of gray cloud crests storming across the sky. The sun was halfway down and in a few more hours it would be dark again. Another day—the sixth since she'd sent Dorsey the note warning him against Mallonee and Jeff's two-faced Melissa.

And Charlotte hadn't had a word from Dorsey in all that time!

She went back to the little table in front of the sofa, hesitated, and then surrendered and poured herself another drink out of the decanter. It was the fourth one she'd taken since noon—too many for a time like this when she needed her wits about her—but her nerves were ready to snap, and she had to have some relief.

Six days without a word from Dorsey!

Six days in which anything and everything could have happened. Mallonee might have ridden in and killed him—but she'd have heard about that, she told herself. Of course she'd have heard about that. But Melissa might be there now, might have been there for days getting Dorsey maneuvered into a position where Mallonee could destroy him.

For any woman who knew what she was doing could wind Dorsey Wilcox around her little finger and keep him there—and he'd never know it. Charlotte had done it herself when she persuaded him to steal Mallonee's money and run away with her because she was tired of Mississippi, tired of her husband, tired of not having the money to buy a new frock when she wanted one. And Melissa McCutcheon, from what Jeff had told her, was a lovely, tempting woman, a woman who knew what she was about when it came to a man.

Charlotte heard Jeff shout outside and got up and looked out the window. He was just swinging down from his horse, and a Negro groom was running up to take the mare back to the stables. Jeff's face was red with the wind but there was a sour twist to his mouth, and she knew his ride hadn't been any more help in taking his mind off Melissa and Dorsey than the brandy had been to her. Their nights were wonderful—but they couldn't fool the days—and they couldn't fool themselves.

He slammed the front door and came down the hall and into the little drawing room where she was sitting, his boots wet and scratched from the brush he'd ridden through, his blue cavalry jacket buttoned up tight and the orange woolen scarf some infatuated woman had knitted for him hanging loose around his throat.

"By hell, there's my lovely lady!" He came across the room and kissed her and the kissing was good, just as it had been on that first night, just as it always was. But it wasn't good enough.

"It's cold enough to strip that brass monkey bare out there today. I hope to God it hasn't done the same thing for me." He put his hand under her chin and tilted her head up so he could look into her face. He laughed softly. "But you wouldn't like that, would you, Charlotte? That wouldn't be a damn bit of good for either one of us."

"You're a fool, my dear," she said, and there was more than a little affection in it. She cupped his hand in hers and dropped her head and kissed his open palm.

"Have a drink, darling." She shoved the decanter across to him and watched him pour a good four fingers of brandy into his glass, weaken it with no more than a tablespoonful of water, and then toss it off as if there'd been no brandy in it at all.

He put the empty glass back on the table and went across to the hearth and stood wide-legged in front of it with his hands behind his back and his head tilted a little to one side as he looked her up and down.

"You haven't heard from Dorsey since I left, I take it?" She shrugged her shoulders. "I haven't heard from Dorsey in over two weeks, but I'm not worried about that."

Charlotte couldn't let him know how worried she was, for she knew he was worried too. Not about Dorsey, but about his damned Melissa—and if he got worried enough he was just fool enough to ride into Springfield to see about her, murder charge or no murder charge. No, regardless of how she felt about it herself, she had to try to pretend to him that everything was all right. She'd be done for if he ever got together with Dorsey—and she and Dorsey would both be ruined if he ever managed to get in touch with Melissa.

"I'm not so damned sure that I'm not."

He pulled the muffler from around his throat and tossed it across the back of a chair, and loosened the buttons on his jacket.

"Something's bound to have happened in there by this time, and I'd like to know what it is."

"What could happen except that Mallonee would ride in and shoot Dorsey? Or your—your wife would be in there now getting it set up for him? That's what you want, isn't it? That's what you said you wanted the afternoon you had me write the note for you. You haven't changed your ideas since then, have you?"

"No—hell, no, they haven't changed." But there was a frown between his eyes that told her he was worrying about that black-haired beauty—and she didn't like it. It wasn't any compliment to have a man keep his mind tied up with some other woman that you'd never seen. It bred a feeling of doubt in a woman, a gnawing, nagging doubt about her own desirability and ability to hold a man.

She didn't want him to look too closely at her face. She got up and went across the room to the windows that looked out over the drive. A closed carriage with the Negro driver shivering in the cold on his high seat up in front was coming up the road, and as she watched, the driver slowed his team of matched grays and swung them into the driveway leading up to the house. She knew the outfit—it was her neighbor, Abbie Lou Posey. If Abbie Lou had been to Springfield she'd have picked up more news and gossip in the few hours she was there than the *Advertiser* could print in a year.

Charlotte hated Abbie's precise, pseudo-genteel little mincing ways and her biting tongue, but there was no doubt that she'd have word of Dorsey. She turned back to the room.

"Abbie Lou's driving in," she told Jeff, "and you're not supposed to be within a thousand miles of Springfield. You'd better hide out until she's gone again."

"That damned clattermouth!" But his eyes brightened a little, and she saw a look of speculation come into his face. "She probably knows more about what's going on in Springfield than we do, though. Damned if I don't think I'll just take a drink into the next room with me and listen to you two chatter together."

It wasn't what she wanted. It wasn't what she wanted at all, but there was no way to tell him that, and no time, either. Abbie's carriage was already swinging in through the porte-cochere and the black butler, Finis, was hurrying across the veranda to open the carriage door for her and bow her inside. She'd be expecting Charlotte to meet her at the door, and she'd be short-tongued and snappish and suspicious if she didn't.

"Go on, then," she said. "But for God's sake don't make a sound. If she ever dreamed that we were here together—" She threw up her arms in a gesture of hopelessness and he laughed and came across to her and kissed her quickly. Then he poured himself a drink and turned toward the library door as she went out to the hall to greet her guest.

Abbie Lou was a sharp-nosed old beldame who should have been hidden away in some wealthy relative's third floor. But instead, she was the richest widow in Greene County, with a gossip's tongue that had broken up more homes and destroyed more reputations than a man could list in a ledger in a long day's work.

Abbie squealed and ran toward Charlotte with her bony arms extended when she saw Charlotte waiting in the doorway.

"Oh, Charlotte!" Her voice was shrill and eager. "I do so feel for you, my dear, and I do think it's just horrible for Dorsey to carry on the way he is—just almost right under your own eyes, you could say, couldn't you? And with a woman whose husband's run away and left her twice, at that. But you must be brave, darling. You must be brave and believe it's all going to work out all right in the end!"

Melissa was in Springfield, then—and Dorsey was unquestionably making a fool of himself over her. She would have given her right arm to keep Jeff from hearing it, for there was no telling what crazy thing he'd do, but she couldn't keep Abbie chattering on the veranda in the cold wind. She shrugged her shoulders and put her arm around the old gossip as she begged her to come into the drawing room where there was a fire.

"I haven't the faintest idea what you're talking about, Abbie." She helped her lay aside her tippet and gloves, and then picked up the decanter and looked at her inquiringly. Abbie Lou had settled herself on the sofa before the fire and her eyes poked at Charlotte and at the room with curiosity, eternally in search of some crumb of something—anything—that could be turned into meal in the gossip mill that she ground.

"Let me give you a little drink to warm you, and then you must tell me all about it. I'll admit I'm fascinated already."

Abbie nodded with a quick, sharp movement, and held out a glass. Charlotte poured in a good measure and then poured one for herself.

"Oh, darling, I—I just don't know how to tell you!" The old woman took Charlotte's hand in one of hers and looked at her with an expression that should have expressed sympathy but was warped into an acid curiosity on her sharp, wizened face. "I've just come from Springfield, and I talked to poor dear Ellamae— she's having such a terrible time with Frank, poor woman; his drinking, you know—and she told me all about this painted, black-haired woman who's come to town pretending she's looking for Jeffrey McCutcheon. Everyone knows he's a vicious, really dangerous man, even if he does come from good people back in Kentucky. And she claims to be his wife, my dear! Just imagine that! And she's snared poor Dorsey into helping her—went right up to him as soon as she got off the stage and started making sheep's eyes at him, they say. Now she's living in that little Gruenther cottage he bought and they say he's down there night and day and I think it's just terrrible for you, Charlotte! I really do! I'm just so sorry for you that I could cry!"

But there were no tears in Charlotte's heart. All she felt was black, blinding rage, a furious desire to get her hands on Dorsey Wilcox. She contrived to look startled and shocked and widened her eyes at Abbie with the look and the gestures of a tender and virtuous wife who had just been stabbed to the heart.

"But I don't understand any of this, Abbie Lou," she protested faintly. "I didn't even know Jeffrey McCutcheon had a wife—and I can't think what she'd be doing in Springfield, or what business Dorsey could have with her. When did she come in? When did Dorsey meet her at the stagecoach?"

"When? Well—" Abbie Lou twisted a little. She didn't like being pinned down on this part of her story, for Melissa hadn't really been there long enough to give it all the depth and flavor of scandal that she loved. "Well, actually, it was only yesterday that she came into Springfield, and of course you've got to believe that it may be perfectly all right. Men do such strange things sometimes. But she came in yesterday on the stage from Rolla and got out right in the middle of the crowd that's always there and flirted her skirts at all of them and said she was looking for her husband, Jeffrey McCutcheon, and asked if anyone could tell where she could find him. Do you really think she could be his wife, Charlotte? My own first thought was that she was some trollop running after him—"

"Why—why, I guess she could be. But you said Dorsey was there to meet her?"

"Oh, yes, my dear. I don't think there was any doubt that he knew she was coming. They say she went right up to him and he was very gallant and very attentive; he can be so nice when he wants to be, you know. And then they went off together with this—this woman hanging on his arm and Dorsey bending down to talk to her and the whole town staring and watching her flirt with him as they went down the sidewalk."

Charlotte felt a sense of resignation dropping down over her. Even with his life at stake—and her own life and welfare hanging on the outcome, too—Dorsey couldn't handle himself around a pretty woman. She'd make a fool of him and he'd be killed by Mallonee as a result of his stupidity.

"And he moved her into his cottage and—and he's been down there with her?"

She wanted to prod the woman along now and get rid of her as fast as she could.

"Oh, he did, Charlotte. He did just that, darling. Moved her in there bag and baggage and sent a supply of groceries down to her and then went back down that evening and stayed there with her until all hours of the night."

"You mean that Ellamae saw all this?"

"Oh, no, she didn't see all of it. But others did, and you know how some people talk. They told Ellamae and she told me and

I just had to tell you because I was sorry for you. And, oh yes, there's one more thing. She was up on the square this noon and she went into Parkinson's store. And then later—I suppose she'd come out of the store and gone up to Dorsey's office without anybody seeing her—she came running down the stairs from his office and almost ran into that little French actress that's been staying at the hotel all winter. Jean Bruillot, she calls herself, and I do know there's been talk about Dorsey hanging around her, too, but I won't say a word about that now, dear, not a word. Well, anyway, this McCutcheon woman and this little French tart met right there at the foot of the stairs and people who were there say that the Bruillot woman looked at her as if she wanted to scratch her eyes out!"

"But they didn't have any trouble—not right there, I mean?"

"Well, not really trouble. Just—looking at each other the way women like that do sometimes, you know. And then McCutcheon's wife turned and practically ran off the square and down to her cottage, and they say the Bruillot woman just rushed up those stairs and then rushed right back down again when she found Dorsey wasn't there. But you just never know what women like that will do, do you, darling? So terrible, I think, to even have to hear about such things, isn't it?"

Charlotte slammed the door the instant Abbie was into her carriage and went back to the drawing room to find Jeff standing in front of the fireplace with his face black and his eyes blazing. He stared at her with one clenched fist rapping on the mantelpiece, and then his voice exploded with a sound like the fierce barking of a volley of guns.

"What the hell's going on in there?" he demanded. "It wasn't just a damned accident that Dorsey met Melissa at the stage and moved her into his house and spent half of last night with her—even if she is a damned beautiful woman, and God knows she's all of that."

"Dorsey's always been a fool for a pretty woman. You know that." She made her voice contemptuous and scornful, and came across the room and put her arms around him.

She pressed against him and let her fingers ruffle the hair at the back of his neck. She'd have all she could do to get Dorsey straightened out and bring him back to his senses—if she could get to him before any more damage was done. But if Jeff went storming in and roiled the waters—She shook her head and refused to think about it.

"Hell, yes, I know that." His body was still stiff and rigid in her arms and the tension was a long way from going out of him. "But what was she doing coming in on a stage from Rolla? And what's become of Mallonee? There's some kind of a game being played in there that I don't understand. I don't like it!"

"Now, darling—" She smoothed his cheek and moved closer against him. "After all, it's your game. It's the one you set up and left for Dorsey to play. You don't think he'd be around her if he thought she was connected with Mallonee, do you? It looks to me as if she's pulled away from Mallonee. He may have been worse hurt in that fight than you thought he was. And if that's the truth, she's probably just gone on and left him and come into Springfield to find you the way she planned to do originally. We're not going to worry about Dorsey—we decided that together. Just leave them alone and one of these days Mallonee will ride in and have it out with Dorsey, and then we'll both be in the clear again."

"Maybe so." He took a deep breath and put his other arm around her and stroked her shoulder. "You're probably right about it, but I don't want anything to go wrong."

"Nothing's going to go wrong. Abbie Lou's told us what we wanted to know, and now we'll sit back and let things work out for us."

He grunted, and when he dropped his arms and turned away toward the table and the decanter, she let him go. She didn't want to spend an extra minute with him, any more than she'd wanted to with Abbie Lou. What she wanted to do was to get into Springfield and get hold of Dorsey. She made up her mind she was going to do it that night—even if she had to go down to his little cottage and pull him out of that woman's arms.

"You'd better go up and change your clothes, hadn't you?" she suggested casually. "We'll be ready for dinner soon."

"I suppose so."

He was still quiet and abstracted, but she didn't care about that. But she didn't want him racing off to Springfield as soon as he found out that she was gone, either.

"Darling," she said, and she put her hand up to her forehead when he turned to look at her. "I think I've had too much brandy. I don't—I just don't feel well at all."

"Too much Abbie Lou, more than likely," he suggested, but she saw his eye take a quick measure of the brandy left in the decanter and then swing back to her.

"I think I'll go up to my room and take a nap," she said, and she tried to make her voice weak. "If I'm not awake by dinnertime, you just go on and eat and don't worry about me. I feel now as if I could sleep straight through till morning."

He stared at her doubtfully, and then he shrugged his shoulders and picked up his muffler from the back of the chair, took several steps toward the door and then turned back to look at her.

"Whatever you want to do, Charlotte," he said. "I know it's been a hard day for you."

He went up the stairs and after a moment she heard his door close behind him. Before the sound had died away, Charlotte was running for a hall closet. She threw on a coat and jammed a hat down over her hair, and ran for the servants' quarters at the back of the house. Finis was just coming through the dining room.

"Finis," she said tensely, "I want Bandit saddled and brought around to the west side of the house—and I want him right now! And if Mr. Jeff asks you where I am any time this evening, you're to tell him that I'm asleep in my room and that I left word that I wasn't to be disturbed under any circumstances. Do you understand that, Finis?"

He bobbed his head, his eyes wide as he stared at her.

"All right, then," she snapped. "Get out here and have a groom saddle that horse. I want him ready in one minute flat."

She hurried back through the hall and out the front door and across the veranda to the porte-cochere. It was almost dark and it would take an hour and a half, even running the horse to death, to get into Springfield. Charlotte slapped nervously at the column of the porte-cochere with the riding whip, and then she saw a groom running toward her with his hand on Bandit's bridle and the big stallion's hoofs kicking up clouds of mud as he came out of the stable yard and into the driveway.

CHAPTER ELEVEN

I T WAS LIKE BEING BALANCED between heaven and hell, Melissa thought. This tight-lipped dread of the swift minutes that brought Wilcox's arrival closer, and the dragging of the hours that separated her from Mallonee. The sun was already down, and it was the hour when there was neither darkness nor daylight. The wind clutching at the corners of the house had taken on an eerie sound that was like a quavering charivari of witches' wailing. Shadows lurked in the corners of the room that the firelight could not reach, and the feeble glow of the double candles on the mantlepiece and on the table was smothered and almost lost in the cloud of the oncoming night.

She had packed her carpetbag and put her blue woolen cloak and a knitted cap on the eiderdown quilt in the bedroom. For tonight—some time tonight, and pray to God it would be early, and soon—she and Mallonee and the Cherokees would be riding out of Springfield with Wilcox as their captive, riding back to Fiddley Flanders's or some other spot Mallonee had selected as the best retreat to use while Dorsey Wilcox was brought to terms.

The back door opened and then closed again and instantly she was on her feet and turned away from the fire and facing the door that led in from the kitchen. If it could only be Mallonee! It seemed to her that her heart stopped beating—and then the door opened and Tahchee and Oconto glided into the room on moccasined feet that were as silent as passing shadows. Her eyes probed the darkness of the room, but they were alone.

"Mallonee?" she said. "Why isn't Mallonee with you?"

"Mallonee come slow—come late." Tahchee shook his head and his eyes seemed to bore into her face. "River up." He jerked his two hands sharply apart to suggest the quick rising of a flash flood. "We cross early this afternoon to hunt out road, see all clear. Then Mallonee and the rest come to river—maybe one, maybe two hours ago. River high. No way for Mallonee to cross. No way for him to get on this side."

"Oh, no—Tahchee!" Melissa's voice showed her disappointment. "But he's got to get here! Wilcox will be here, and—"

Tahchee threw up his hand to stop her, and she recognized the proud, iron-hard dignity in him.

"Tahchee here," he said grimly. "And Oconto here. We stay here until Mallonee comes."

"He is coming, then? He will be able to ford the river?"

"Not cross at ford on road. Too deep, too high, too fast. Ride downstream many miles—fifteen, twenty maybe. Bridge there where he can cross. Then ride back into Springfield. Ride here."

"Oh, but Tahchee—he won't be here till morning, then!"

Tahchee shook his head, his face unchanging.

"Not too long, I think. We talk to him across river two hours ago. He start then and he ride fast. He be here in, maybe, two more hours. We stay here, watch for Wilcox, till he comes."

"But you can't do that, Tahchee." The thought of the talk she had heard in Wilcox's office that afternoon came back to her, and the room seemed to spin in a momentary dizziness of doubt and hopelessness. "Listen to me, Tahchee—listen carefully. Last night you heard Wilcox say that he'd be here without his guards. You heard him, didn't you?"

The Cherokee nodded without speaking, his eyes suddenly cold and watchful and wary.

"I slipped into his office this afternoon—he didn't know I was there—and I heard him talking to one of his guards. He's going to have them with him tonight, Tahchee! He was lying when he said he wouldn't bring them! He's almost sure that I'm working with Mallonee, and I think he suspects some sort of an ambush, either now or later."

Melissa took a deep breath, nerving herself to the act of sending these tribesmen who were her only possible protectors away from her.

"You can't stay here with me. I'll have to try to handle him the best way I can. You'll have to ride out of here and meet Mallonee. Find him, wherever he is, and tell him that Wilcox will be guarded tonight just as he always is—just as he was last night. Mallonee's got to know! If he doesn't, he'll ride straight into a trap!"

Tahchee's right hand slapped down hard upon his left forearm in a gesture of sudden anger. He barked a sharp volley of sound at Oconto and the short, barrel-chested Cherokee's face turned hard as he answered in a shower of speech whose meaning Melissa could not even guess.

"Say whatever you've got to say in English!" Melissa's nervousness and doubt flowered in a sudden flare of anger. "I'm in this just as much as you are, just as much as Mallonee is! Whatever you've got to say, I want to hear it."

"Say little. Say nothing hurt Mallonee's woman." For an instant it seemed to her that there was a spark of amusement in Tahchee's merciless eyes. "We say Oconto go back, find Mallonee. Tell him. I stay here. Wait outside. Watch where Wilcox's warriors hide. Tell him when he comes in. Then, after he here—" His hands finished the sentence with the gesture of wringing a chicken's head from its body.

Relief poured through her at the knowledge that she was not to be left completely alone with Wilcox—not after what she had promised him the night before. He would be hard to curb, but that didn't matter now. Not if Tahchee were just outside and Mallonee was on his way to her.

It was not until they were gone that the sudden thought came to her that no matter what Wilcox might do, Tahchee would be powerless to interfere. For Tahchee's first loyalty was to Mallonee, and if he revealed himself before Mallonee and the others arrived, they would be betrayed; and their lives—when they did come—would be worth less than the snap of a finger.

A cold numbness seemed to close down on her. She crossed the room to the fireplace and let its heat beat out upon her. But the cold would not go away. It would never go away until she was safe with Mallonee again.

CHAPTER TWELVE

D INNER COULDN'T HAVE BEEN a worse meal if he'd supped with the devil, Jeffrey reflected sourly. Finis had told him that Charlotte had gone to bed and had sent down word that she wasn't to be disturbed under any conditions. The slave was uneasy and afraid even then, for his eyes shifted away from Jeff's cold glare and his voice had lost the warm, rolling boom that was as much a part of it as its soft-slurred accent. But Jeff brushed the casual impression of the slave's agitation aside impatiently.

Ever since Abbie Lou had rattled out her story, he had been jumpy and uneasy, plagued by a vague doubt. Certainly, he told himself irritably, Dorsey hadn't heard of Melissa from him. What he and Melissa had had between them—and God knew he'd made that little enough—it had been their affair and no business of Dorsey's. And there'd been no hint of her in the note he'd dictated to Charlotte. He'd seen the note himself, and seen Charlotte go straight out of the library to find a groom to carry it into town.

But there wasn't a doubt that Dorsey had guessed a part of the truth, some way or other. If he hadn't guessed it, or been told about it, he'd never have met her and welcomed her there at the stage. And the matter of her arrival on the stage was another knot in the skein of confusion. But that would have to wait.

He picked half-heartedly at the meal Finis set before him. But there was enough port wine to correct any deficiency—wine tamped down with three glasses of brandy at the table, and two more after he went back to the drawing room.

There was a puzzle in it, but he couldn't get it to come straight. Staring at the fire, he blew cigar smoke at the flames on the hearth, poured another drink, and tried to work it out again. But the problem was as impregnable as a globe of polished granite. There was no flaw in it.

There wasn't any way Dorsey could have known…

He'd had no word from the three renegades who'd run away early in the skirmish at the state line. Jeff was sure of that, for he'd caught up with them at a little crossroads store north of the Missouri line and found them still whitefaced and shaken, afraid to go on and determined not to go back. He'd paid them what he'd promised them, and they'd turned tail and struck for the Indian Territory, where they'd be out of reach until Mallonee and Wilcox came to the end of the bloody quarrel that had flared up.

Whatever Dorsey had heard about Melissa hadn't come from them.

And there was no other living soul who could have told him! No one else knew the truth of that affair. No one except Charlotte—

The thought shook him as if it had been a stone wall he'd crashed into at full gallop. He hadn't probed his way through to that particular point before. But there was no reason in it! He tried to dismiss the idea.

But slowly, reluctantly, he began to fit the chips and pieces of it together. The way she'd come into his room that first night, naked except for the satin lounging robe she'd worn, and the way she'd thrown that aside as soon as she was inside the door. It had pleased his vanity then, but in this new light of suspicion it seemed to him that he was emerging as a gullible, empty-headed fool. It was beyond belief that _she'd selected that particular night to surrender to him through sheer coincidence.

He slammed his fist down on the arm of the chair as a lightning flash of memory reminded him that he'd talked of riding into Springfield to see Dorsey that night. And she'd rejected the idea without seeming to think twice about it. He jerked himself to his feet and sent his cigar spinning into the fire. After a minute, he began to pace up and down the room with his hands locked behind his back and his mind racing.

He'd written Dorsey a note that told no more than he'd wanted to tell. And then Charlotte had taken the note—he forced his mind to a minute review of her actions—and had said she was going to call a groom and send the note to Dorsey. And a little later he'd heard a horse come up, stop, and then gallop off.

But there'd been a good fifteen minutes between the time he left the library and the time he'd heard the horse gallop away: time enough for Charlotte to have done anything. Time enough for her to tear up his note and write Dorsey an entirely different one—a true one!

He stopped in his tracks as the truth battered its way into his brain. Then he was out of the door and taking the steps three at a time as he raced toward the door of Charlotte's bedroom.

He kicked her door open, driving it so viciously that it swung in a half-circle and slammed hard against the wall behind it as the latch splintered out of the door frame. The room was dark, with only the light from the candles in the hall sconces to light it.

"Charlotte!" His voice was a savage blast of fury. "Charlotte—damn you—where are you?"

He plunged across the room toward her bed, but his hands found nothing except a silken-smooth counterpane and pillows still as round and plump as fresh loaves of bread. He threw his arms wide, sweeping over the bed from side to side, but it was as empty and untouched as if it had never been used. He whirled, trying to see the rest of the room, but the darkness was too deep. Cursing, gasping for breath, he ran out into the hall and tore one of the thick white candles out of its sconce and whirled back into the room again. He could see now—holding the candle high above his head and feeling the hot, melted wax dripping down upon his hand and wrist—he could see every crack and corner of the place.

Charlotte was gone! For an instant it seemed to him that his brain was locked in a vise.

Suddenly his mind cleared, wiped clear of the doubt and the confusion that had manacled him. If Charlotte had gone to Dorsey, he had no choice now except to go to Melissa. For if Dorsey was a jackal, Charlotte was a tiger—and between them Melissa's life was worth nothing.

He jumped for the door of his own room and scooped up hat, jacket and scarf. There was a pair of saddle-holstered dragoon pistols on top of his chest of drawers, and there was always powder and shot in his saddlebags.

He scooped up the guns and raced down the stairs. Finis had heard the commotion and run out into the hall with his face gray with fear. He started to speak and in the same instant Jeff's full weight slammed into him. He stumbled backward and Jeff's fingers closed down on his throat, jerking him upright as he began to fall.

"Charlotte saddled a horse and went to Springfield, didn't she? Don't lie to me now or I'll kill you. How long's she been gone? Since before dinner—while I was upstairs?"

The slave's head jerked in a stiff nod. Staring eyes bulging out of his head, he lifted his arm in an awkward gesture that managed to indicate the outside door and the porte-cochere beyond.

So she'd been gone at least two hours, Jeff thought savagely. Two hours, and God only knew what hell's broth she'd brewed for Melissa in that time. He ran for the back door, closest entrance to the stables.

He would pay out Charlotte and Dorsey for the debt he owed them once he was in Springfield.

If he could get there in time!

CHAPTER THIRTEEN

JEAN BRUILLOT HAD GONE far beyond anger, far beyond
doubt. During the two days and a night that had passed
since Melissa had come to Springfield, her original curiosity had
grown into fear, and then panic, so that now, on the late evening
of the second day, her fury had become completely wild.

She'd been afraid of something like this for a long time, she
realized bitterly. Ever since she'd come to realize that Dorsey
didn't really want to be done with Charlotte, and marry her—in
spite of all his promises, in spite of the fact that she'd been his
woman now for almost a year. She'd waited for him the night
before—but he hadn't come to her.

She'd taken too much to drink, waiting for him, so that the
next morning her mouth was parched and dry and her head
was a throbbing agony of blinding pain. She'd started drinking
again, that morning, to shut out the pain and to shut out the fear
that was closing down on her like a vise. And in the afternoon,
with the cold wind beating at her and the bleak sky looking like a
shroud, she'd seen Melissa—seen her, and known on the instant
that the peril was even more real than she had imagined. She'd
known then that she'd have to get rid of Melissa.

Back at the hotel, she'd left word with the clerk to send
Dorsey up to her as soon as he came in. And in her room she'd
got the long-bladed dirk she'd bought in Havana out of her trunk
and put it on the bed beside her pillow and looked at it as she
drank and drank again and waited for Dorsey. If Dorsey would
only tell her—

But it wouldn't make any difference what he told her—for a woman like Melissa could take him away from her with the flick of a finger.

She touched the knife, and waited for his footsteps in the hall outside her room.

Dorsey Wilcox came into the hotel lobby just at sundown, with Loosh Maggard at his side. Before they had gone ten steps, the door opened again and his second bodyguard, Arch Ritland, came in with a rush, swept the lobby with hard eyes, and shot a quick look into the adjoining barroom. Then he went across the room and dropped down into a chair so placed that he could command both the front door and the foot of the stairway.

The potbellied desk clerk had been waiting for Wilcox with eager anticipation in his eyes.

"Mr. Wilcox—oh, Mr. Wilcox!" His words quavered up and down nervously. Two of the traveling drummers who had been working the town all day glanced up curiously as he motioned Wilcox over to the desk.

He leaned forward, cupping his hand around his mouth, his whisper sharp and conspiratorial in Wilcox's ear. "Miss Bruillot wants to see you mighty bad, Mr. Wilcox. Left word with me to tell you early this afternoon, and she's sent down twice to know if you'd come in yet."

"Hell's bells! I don't want to—" He caught himself and his mouth clamped shut as if to cut off the words. "All right, Manny. I'll see her."

He'd hoped he'd be able to slip in and out of the hotel without running into Jean Bruillot. Beyond any doubt she'd heard of Melissa by this time, and that—and the fact that for the first time in months he hadn't gone into her apartment the night before—would almost certainly have driven her into one of those white-faced, whip-tongued rages that he'd come to dread. But this was one time she was going to take it, for this was a matter of life and death—his life, and Mallonee's death.

He stamped up the stairs with a frown twisting his face, and at the top of the steps he saw that her door was half open and that she was standing in the opening, her red hair caught in a flowing mass at the back of her neck, the black lace negligee she wore revealing far more than it concealed. Four months ago he'd have gone half crazy at seeing her like that, but the novelty of it was gone now. Most of the time—except when her tricks drove him wild—he wanted to get rid of her. But she had her claws into him and she wasn't going to let go unless he hammered her loose. It wasn't going to be easy to talk to her now.

She was silent, but her eyes held him, defying him to turn into his own room, away from her. He squared his shoulders and jerked his head toward the door of his room.

"You wait for me in there, Loosh," he commanded. "Help yourself to a drink if you want one. I won't be long."

Her eyes turned hot and furious at his final words, but she turned back into the apartment without a word and he followed her inside and kicked the door shut behind him.

He could see her much better now, in this room where the candles were gleaming, and in spite of his anger and indecision he felt a sudden tightening in his lungs at the artfully disclosed pattern of white flesh and her body half seen and half suggested through the open lace work of the black negligee. But then he thought of Mallonee—his hard fists and the hungry devil that was always lurking in his eyes—and he was suddenly frantic to be free of this vixen. He had to see Melissa and force from her the information that would release him from this agony of fear and uncertainty.

"Manny said you wanted to see me." It was an effort to make his voice hard and abrupt and uncompromising, but he did it. "I haven't got much time."

"Oh, so you haven't got much time!" She had whirled around to face him. "You mean you haven't much time for me, don't you? Or maybe you don't have any time for me, since Jeffrey McCutcheon's wife came to town? Is that what you mean? Damn you, Dorsey, is that what you're trying to tell me?"

It was a relief to let the anger come out. "I don't know what you've heard about her and I don't give a damn, but I'll tell you this—she's got information I've got to have, and I'm going to get it. I don't care whether you like it or not. This is something that's got to be done."

She half turned away as if to avoid something that had disgusted her and then swung back viciously. "Don't you know that a woman like that can make an utter fool of you, Dorsey? Don't you know that she'll get ten times as much out of you as you'll get out of her? If she's got information that you need, the chances are she's trying to get more right now. If she's a danger to you, why don't you kill her and forget about it? She wouldn't be the first one you've killed. I know that much about you, and it's not all I know, either!"

"Maybe you know too damn much."

He was cold, suddenly as cold as if an icy hand had fastened itself on the back of his neck. He couldn't think, couldn't remember, what he had let slip to this smooth-skinned devil in front of him. He had probably told her far too much.

His nails bit into his palms as his hands stiffened into fists and he fought for control and sanity again. She was bluffing.

"Look, Jean—" There was a wire-tight thread in his voice, but he fought to hold it steady. "Let's don't start clawing at each other now. I've got hell's own load of troubles on my shoulders, and Melissa McCutcheon's part of the trouble. I've got to play along with her till I find out what I've got to know. She doesn't mean a damn thing to me outside of that, and whatever I have to do with her isn't going to hurt you. It's going to help you, Jean, because it's going to help both of us. Can't you see that?"

"See it!" She took a deep breath and her breasts rose and fell. "How could I see it? I don't even know what you're talking about, and I don't think you do either. But I'm going to tell you one thing, Dorsey, and I want you to listen to me." She took a quick step forward, and the black negligee fell open as her hands came up and fastened upon the lapels of his coat. "I've been true to you because I loved you and because you promised to marry me. But I'm not going to take this much from you, Dorsey!"

Her face was twisted with fury, and her hands had knotted themselves into hard fists that pounded frantically against his chest. "If you don't get rid of that woman I'll kill her—and kill you, too! I'm not going to take any more. I'll—"

He shoved her away from him roughly and slapped her hard, twice, his hand striking down and back in a vicious double arc that smashed her lips back against her teeth and brought a trickle of blood from the corner of her mouth.

Jean caught her breath, her eyes aghast, staring at him, and then she screamed and he struck her again, with his fist this time, and she went back and down on the faded carpet, the black negligee torn half off and sharp gusts of pain gasping out between her battered lips.

"Damn you!" His voice grated like steel against stone. "Don't you tell me what you're going to do or not do!" He took a threatening step toward her, and she sobbed and threw up a hand to fend him off and tried to push herself across the carpet and away from him.

"Don't! Don't do it, Dorsey—"

He loomed over her, shoulders half bent, fists clenched, arms swinging forward. The mood to kill her, to put an end to her once and for all was screaming wind in him—but there was the cold hand of fear upon his back, too. He sucked in a deep breath and felt his body relax a little and knew with a sudden sickening horror that he had already gone too far. But there was nothing to do but brazen it out if he could.

"All right," he said harshly. "Just remember that what you got tonight was just a sample. You keep your nose out of what I do. Let Melissa McCutcheon alone. You understand that?"

She nodded dumbly, her eyes furious and inscrutable upon his face, her hands trying to pull the black negligee up so that it would cover her body. His eyes threatened her, and he started to speak again and then grunted and turned on his heel and stalked out of the room. The door slammed behind him.

After a long minute, Jean got to her feet and went to the mirror above the dressing table and touched the blood upon her face with the tips of her fingers and then poured water into a bowl and began to wash the blood away. When it was done, she dressed herself, as carefully and meticulously as if she had been going to a ball. She took the Cuban dirk out of her handbag and balanced it in her hand for a moment, considering it. Then she lifted her skirt and slipped it inside the top of her stocking, along her thigh, where the garter would hold it tight and firm.

She started toward the door, but when she was halfway there she turned and went back to the liquor cabinet and took out a decanter and poured a glass half full of whisky. She drank it as steadily as if it had been water, and when it was gone she closed the liquor cabinet carefully and went back to the door again. The knife was cool and hard and slim against her thigh.

Melissa McCutcheon would be in her cottage not ten minutes' walk away, waiting for Dorsey Wilcox.

CHAPTER FOURTEEN

J EAN MOVED VERY STEALTHILY, for there was not a sound until the door of the cottage flew open, with the cold wind rushing in, and Melissa whirled and saw the red-haired woman standing just inside the door. For an instant there was no fear in her, for she had been so terrified by the knowledge that Wilcox would arrive before Mallonee could reach her, that she felt relief when she saw that it was the woman. She had been so afraid that it was Wilcox.

But that was only for an instant. For this woman hated her. It was in her eyes and in the twist of her mouth and in the explosive, cat-like tautness of her body. Her hands, half lifted away from her sides, twisted and writhed and knotted themselves into fists.

"What do you—what do you want here?" Melissa's voice broke and she caught her breath, and then suddenly anger flared in her. "Get out of my house! Get out and get out now—"

"Your house?" The red-headed woman's voice was brutally insulting. "When did this get to be your house, Melissa McCutcheon? The minute Dorsey Wilcox moved you into it, without ever telling you that he'd bought it for me? The minute that he came to you last night? Why don't you tell me?"

"Bought it for you—" The implications of the phrase jolted into her with the smashing impact of a clenched fist driven into her face. "But then you're Dorsey Wilcox's wife! You're Charlotte Sherwood, from Mississippi—"

"I'm Jean Bruillot."

The name meant nothing to Melissa, and she shook her head in a dazed bewilderment. She saw the woman's eyes blaze into a brighter anger, as if the very fact of not knowing her was an offense.

"You haven't heard of Jean Bruillot then? And you wouldn't have cared if you had! But I'm going to be his wife one of these days—and you'll not take him away from me!" Her hand dived in under her skirt and when it came up again there was a lean, needle-pointed dagger in it.

She came in a rush then, like an animal, with insane eyes and her mouth twisted back into a snarl and the dagger driving like the pointed head of a striking snake. Melissa screamed and dodged to one side, twisting desperately so that the sofa was between them. The attack had come so completely without warning, that her mind was stunned and her body seemed to be too heavy to ever let her defend herself. She could feel the muscles of her thighs jerking uncontrollably and her breath was locked tight, choking her, hard and brittle and swollen in her throat.

"Get away from me!" Melissa realized that the words were a strained whisper, as if this thing that was happening were some terrible secret that must be hidden away from the world. "I don't want Dorsey Wilcox! I don't want him, I tell you—"

"And you won't have him, either!"

The Frenchwoman darted around the sofa. The knife flickered in the firelight and Melissa knocked it aside and fell back two steps, her face white and her black eyes wide and horrified.

The red-haired woman struck again and then she had Melissa pinned hard against the table, her left hand clawing at Melissa's eyes and the dagger rushing up in a flashing, murderous arc.

Melissa screamed again, dissolved in horror, the scream pitched on the high, hysterical notes of desperation. Then she was grappling with this wildcat, clawing at her wrists and forcing the knife away, kicking at her and trying to drive her off.

The heavy odor of the musky perfume Jean Bruillot wore was heavy in Melissa's nostrils, and the illogical thought blazed for an instant in her mind that it was ludicrous that she should be struggling for her life against a woman she had seen only once before, while the fragrance of the stranger's perfume swirled up about them like a haunted mist.

The woman's hand caught in the collar of Melissa's dress, ripping it open down to the waist, her clawing fingers tearing the lace-edged camisole away, gouging long, bloody strips of flesh out of Melissa's shoulders and breasts, so that now she fought half naked, with the blood pouring down across her body. The back of her hand slashed Melissa across the mouth and the red-painted, long-nailed fingers were digging into her throat, choking her, forcing her back helplessly against the table.

A dark blur was widening in Melissa's mind, whirling faster and faster as it blotted out her will and her strength. She could feel her sweat-slick fingers slipping on the woman's wrist—

Somewhere, somewhere far away and behind her, she heard a door slammed hard against a wall and a man's voice shouting something in a language that was strange and wild and barbarous. The red-headed woman screamed like a wounded cat as a great shadow loomed up between Melissa and the light. The woman screamed and whirled, and the dark haze that had spread down over Melissa's eyes dissolved just enough for her to see that Tahchee was there in the room and was spinning the woman away from her.

The Indian's hand lashed out at the red-haired woman, and her head jerked back and showed blood dripping from her mouth. The door crashed open again as other men came through it and in the instant that Tahchee whirled to look behind him the Frenchwoman lunged forward and drove the dagger straight into his body, just below the heart.

He seemed to stiffen for an instant, and his swarthy face twisted and then hardened into a savage mask. He lunged toward her, the knife hilt rising from his chest. Back by the doorway a gun barked and then another joined it.

Tahchee's head tilted back as his arms flew up and then he staggered forward across the room, his knees buckling beneath him until he struck a chair. He went down across it and lay still.

For an instant, it seemed as if the red-haired woman was going to follow him. Then she turned, and her hand went up to her throat. Eyes bulging, she tried to speak, but before she could her body drooped and the hand fell away from her throat. As she fell, Melissa saw the round, black bullet hole there, just where the base of her throat met the first lifting curve of her breasts.

Slowly, Melissa turned her head toward the door, toward the furious echoing of the shots.

Dorsey Wilcox and Loosh Maggard were standing there, their guns smoking in their hands—and a look of incredulous horror was growing in Wilcox's face.

CHAPTER FIFTEEN

I T WAS AN HOUR PAST DARK when Charlotte Sherwood rode into Springfield. The stallion, Bandit, was almost done in, for she'd shown him no mercy. His bit was white with foam and he was trembling and wheezing when she pulled him up in front of the hotel. The street was empty, for the wind had come up again and it was cold and miserable outside, with rain and sleet in the air.

She ran into the hotel, her riding whip still in her hand. Two fat drummers in gaudy vests who were playing cards in front of the fireplace laid down their cards and turned to stare at her with appraising eyes. The room clerk bobbed up behind the desk and as he smirked at her he adjusted a violently purple and yellow tie.

"Why, good evening, Miss Wilcox! Good evening! Didn't look to see you out on a night like this." He was all fawning smiles and twisting hands and devouring, prying curiosity.

"I want to see Mr. Wilcox. Is he up in his room?"

"Well, now," he leaned forward confidentially. "As a matter of fact, he ain't there right now. But if you'd like to set here and wait for him I'll get hold of one of the boys and start him out after Mr. Wilcox."

"You know where he is then?" she demanded.

"Why—why, no, not for sure, I don't." His face turned red and his Adam's apple bobbed up and down. "I just thought I could have one of the boys look around for him some. It ain't—" he snickered nervously—"it ain't so big a town he'd have many places he could be."

But she was in no mood to sit and wait while some por-
ter ran through the rain to tell Dorsey that she was looking for
him. He wasn't in his office. She knew that, for she'd ridden
along that side of the square on her way to the hotel and there'd
been no light in his window. And it wasn't likely he'd be in one
of the bars—not when he could be with a woman like Melissa
McCutcheon.

She dug down into the pocket of her riding coat and found
the flat leather pocket case filled with St. Louis bank notes she
always kept there. She'd known for a long time that anything
could happen, any time, and she never left the house after they
came to Missouri without carrying at least a thousand dollars
with her. And there was more in the same bank in St. Louis that
had issued the bank notes. She'd wormed it out of Dorsey, little
by little, for she'd made up her mind from the start that whatever happened to him she would never be helpless and poverty-
stricken again.

She worked a ten-dollar note free from the others and
brought her hand up with the note half out of her palm. She saw
Manny's eyes flick down at it and then jerk back up to her face
again, and he licked his lips as if he knew what was coming, but
didn't know what he was going to do when the decision was put
up to him.

"Manny," she said firmly, and her voice was as flat and
uncompromising as a jailhouse door, "you're going to tell me just
exactly where Dorsey is right now." She threw up her hand to
shut off his stammering protests, and then let the hand open so
that he could see the bank note she was offering him.

He lifted one skinny hand and wiped the sweat away from
his lip.

"He'd kill me sure, if I said anything—" he whispered. But
he took a deep breath and swallowed hard and then his fingers
grabbed at the bank note. He leaned far forward and put up one
hand to shield his mouth and muffle his words.

"He's down to that Gruenther cottage he bought, down the other side of Jordan's Branch. Him an' Loosh Maggard an' Arch Ritland. But don't let on I told you! Don't let him know—"

But she was away from the desk and across the lobby and out through the door before he had the last words out of his mouth. She'd known it, and yet she had prayed that it wouldn't be so. Dorsey was with Melissa, and he'd been with her the night before. He was a fool wherever a woman was concerned!

She didn't know what she was going to do, except that she was going down there and going to get him away from Melissa and make him see what immediate danger was facing them. She swung up on Bandit and realized that he was still trembling and that he couldn't go much farther. She cut at his flank with the whip and he threw up his head and swung around in the street, heading back toward the square and the road that led north toward the cottage.

There was no one in sight as they went around the courthouse and started down the sharp-sloping hill that would take them to the ford and the footbridge across Jordan's Branch.

She could see a light in the windows of the cottage as Bandit splashed his way across the stream. She cut at him again with the quirt and then she saw the door of the cottage slam open and a yellow square of light fall on the shallow front steps and two men ran in through the door. Suddenly there were two shots that seemed to shatter the night. Her heart stopped. The night shut down again, and she wanted to turn and run—but she had to know what had happened.

She jerked Bandit to one side, slipped out of the saddle, and began to run down the rutted road toward the cottage. She was less than fifty feet away when she saw another man run up out of the darkness and go crashing in through the door, and as the light hit him she recognized him as Arch Ritland. She wheeled off the road, frantic with terror now, and fought her way through the rain-soaked bushes and underbrush until she was outside a lighted window. One of the shutters was open, and she pushed her face up to the glass and looked inside.

There were three candles burning, and the air was gray with gunsmoke and a black-haired woman, naked to the waist, was half collapsed over a table with blood pouring out of deep cuts on her face and shoulders. Another woman, a red-haired woman, was crumpled up on the floor. Two feet beyond her an Indian in a long hunting shirt and a red and yellow turban was sprawled face down across an overturned chair, and there was a pool of blood on the floor around his waist.

For a second the room seemed to whirl and dive in front of her, and she thought she was going to faint. Her face was fiery hot and then icy cold. She knew that she was pounding her clenched fist helplessly against the window frame.

She took a deep breath to steady herself and looked into the room again. Dorsey and Loosh Maggard, standing close together, each had a gun, and Arch Ritland was half a dozen feet away, staring at them as if he couldn't believe his eyes, his own gun half out of its holster. She saw Dorsey shake his head and then his hand came up and he wiped his forehead. Loosh Maggard looked at him and his mouth twisted and he dropped his gun back into its holster.

"Well, Dorsey," he said, and there was a sort of vengeful triumph in his voice, "you killed her, didn't you? I guess that kind of makes us even on that other thing we were talkin' about today."

"I killed her?"

Dorsey's hand came down and his head jerked like a puppet on a string and his teeth gnawed at his lower lip.

"I killed her—why, damn it, Loosh, I shot at that damn Cherokee!" His arm jerked spasmodically toward the Indian sprawled across the chair. "I didn't shoot at Jean! I wouldn't shoot at her! You're the one that killed her, God damn you! You're the one—"

"I'm not the one." Maggard's voice had changed so that it was flat and deadly. She saw Dorsey's mouth jerk and his eyes widen in the beginning of fear. "I hit what I aim at, Dorsey—an' I shot at the Injun." His hand came down and touched the butt of his holstered gun. Dorsey's eyes followed the hand as if it had been a coiling snake. "You never could hit a bull with a fryin' pan, an' you know it. I shot at the Injun, an' I hit him. Maybe you shot at him too, I don't know—but if you did you missed him an' hit your woman instead."

And so the woman on the floor was Jean Bruillot! Charlotte looked at her and felt even a little pity for her. But she knew that because of the way that she'd died, at Dorsey's hands, she'd managed to destroy everything that Charlotte and Dorsey had planned.

That this time Dorsey had gone too far. He'd killed before, but he never had killed a woman. He hadn't meant to do it, but that didn't make any difference. For now Loosh Maggard and Arch Ritland and, worst of all, the black-haired woman, Melissa McCutcheon, knew it. She was Dorsey's enemy—she was the one who'd finally lead him to his death.

It hit Dorsey just as it had Charlotte, for his face went gray and he looked around from one to the other with a sort of despair in his face.

"By God—" he said, and he stopped and then started again. "By God, we'll never know who did it." His eyes twisted around toward Loosh and Arch and there was a desperate, pleading look in them. "I'll pay you," he said huskily. "I'll pay both of you to keep your mouths shut. I'll make it right with you."

"I reckon you will." Loosh laughed harshly. "I'd figured that all out before you spoke up an' said so. But you can't buy her off, Dorsey—" His head jerked toward Melissa. "There's bad blood between you two. You better figure out what you're goin' to do with her, and damn fast, too. We ain't far from the square, so there's plenty there that heard this shooting."

"We'll get these bodies out of here," Dorsey said desperately. "Get them out and tell whoever comes that we were shooting at a stray dog—"

"You ain't got time to get 'em out, Dorsey." Loosh's voice was as inflexible as steel. "We got to get out of here right now. But what are you goin' to do with her? You goin' to take her with you, or gun her down like you done the other one?"

Charlotte saw Dorsey's eyes widen in horror and he shook his head and jammed his gun down hard into his holster.

"Hell, no, Loosh! Not another one! Not after—" he seemed to gather himself together and his jaw hardened and she knew that he was thinking of Mallonee, of the fact that the danger from Mallonee was even greater than the danger of discovery and that Melissa was the only key he had that would turn the lock upon that threat.

"We'll take her and go," he said abruptly. "I've got a place down south of here, down on the Finley. We'll take her down there."

He looked around the room, and then turned and hurried into the bedroom. When he came out he had a blue woolen cloak and a knitted woman's cap in his hand. He jerked the woman away from the table and when she struggled he struck her across the face with the back of his hand. She gasped and would have fallen if he hadn't held her, but he threw the cloak around her and jammed the cap down over her head and began to half pull and half carry her toward the door.

"Arch," he commanded, "you and Loosh kite up to the livery stable and get four horses saddled and down to where Jordan curves south as fast as you can. I'll take her on there and wait for you."

He shoved her out through the door and Loosh and Arch came after him and turned back up the hill toward town, both of them going in a stumbling run. Dorsey and the woman turned away from the road, toward the west, down toward the vacant land where there weren't any roads or any houses.

Charlotte had an impulse to run after him, but she knew it was too late for that now. Dorsey Wilcox was done for. Today, or maybe tomorrow, pr maybe a week from now—they'd catch up with him. And she wasn't going to be caught with him.

There was a stage that left for Rolla at midnight, and Bandit could carry her another ten miles up the pike, to the first stage station. She could slip out of Springfield and catch the stage there, and that would be the last they'd ever see of Charlotte Sherwood. She touched the leather case full of bank notes in her pocket, and it was cool and firm and comforting. There were more waiting for her in the bank at St. Louis. She began to smile a little, thinking about them.

Dorsey had given them to her—but there wouldn't be any Dorsey to worry her when she started to spend them.

CHAPTER SIXTEEN

IT HAD TAKEN THE DEVIL'S OWN TIME for Mallonee and his tribesmen to find their way down the brink of the flood-swollen river to the bridge that would carry them across it. The sun was down and the freezing rain and sleet that had come with the dusk tore at them with freezing whips before they were across the stream and headed north toward Springfield again.

Even at the best, Mallonee thought savagely, they were a good two hours from Melissa's cottage, and Dorsey Wilcox would most certainly be there long before they could arrive. He damned himself for delaying the start from Fiddley Flanders's—but it was done, and there was nothing to do now except to push the horses hard in the race against time.

The darkness, laced with the slanting lances of the sleet and hail, closed in around them as they rode north across a stretch of country that was strange to them. The overgrown trail led them through wide stretches of virgin oak and elm and hickory, broken here and there by tiny clearings hacked out of the forest where there were tiny, tightly shuttered log cabins and packs of yelping hounds to run out and bay and snarl at them. Sometimes a light flashed up in a window as they rode by, but there was no time to stop—no time for anything except for the pitiless, exhausting drive toward Springfield and Melissa.

They had come some fifteen miles across country when the trail widened into a narrow, rutted, frozen road. They swung into it and tried to push the steaming horses to a faster pace. A little beyond the junction of the trail and the road, just as they were coming into a heavy patch of ice covered timber, Mallonee heard a screech owl cry out twice, a common enough sound if it had not been for the eerie note that seemed to cling to the end of each quavering call. His head jerked up when he heard it, for this was a Cherokee tribal call, a signal used by tribesmen when they were in enemy country. And yet there was no reason on God's earth why anyone should be there to hail them.

The Cherokees riding behind him checked their horses, and Mallonee's hand went to the pistol at his belt and whipped the gun up out of its holster. Riding slowly ahead, eyes searching the shapeless form of the timber ahead of him, he answered the call, the gun balanced warily in his hand. There was the crackling of frozen mud and ice under a horse's hoofs and then Oconto rode out into the trail. His horse was covered with foam and sweat and the steam from its nostrils was a white cloud in the windy vacuum of the freezing air.

"*Kah-ho-tee-na*—greetings to my brother!"

He rode forward and Mallonee dropped the gun back into its holster and kicked his horse up alongside while the others pressed in curiously at his back.

"What in the hell are you doing here?" he demanded harshly. "I sent you and Tahchee to stay with the woman—"

"Tahchee with her. Send me meet you. All bad. Your woman hear Wilcox say he bring his men with him tonight. Much fighting then, I think. Or maybe too late for fighting when we get there."

"Great God!" The shock of knowing Melissa's real danger, piled atop the delay, brought the words out of his mouth in a furious despair that was more prayer than epithet. "She's there alone with him, then! And nobody but Tahchee there to look after her—and three men against him. They weren't there when you left?"

The Cherokee shook his head.

"Woman alone when I left. Tahchee hide outside. Watch so he see where they go and tell you when you come."

It seemed to Mallonee then, for a long, black moment, that defeat had him by the throat, and a blind rage swept up inside him. He called to the men behind him, and then he was lashing his horse and driving him into a headlong gallop and the others were thundering close behind him while the trees whipped by swiftly. Nothing mattered except getting to Melissa before Wilcox could hurt her.

They roared across the hail-lashed, empty square of Springfield, down a little slope and across a stream hidden in darkness; and then Oconto grunted and Mallonee looked ahead and saw light glowing through the windows of a little cottage to the right of the road. The thought flashed through his mind that Tahchee should have heard them coming—should have been at the stream to meet them—but there was no one, anywhere, and they drove in toward the house with their guns out.

A dozen feet short of the house, Mallonee threw himself out of the saddle and ran toward the house. The door of the cottage was gaping open and he went through it like a mad bull.

"Melissa!" he cried. "Melissa—where are you!"

He caught himself then and whirled to one side with his gun raking the room, for he'd caught a glimpse of the two bloody bodies sprawled grotesquely on the floor. Tahchee—and the woman must be Melissa! His boot heels echoed against the emptiness as he ran toward the body. He dropped on his knees beside her and his hand was under her head when the shock of realization struck him. It was not Melissa!

She was a young woman, red-headed, and she'd been pretty once—but that night she was a sight to shake the heart in a man. Her hair had fallen down around her face and blood had dried on her face and chin and throat and there was a raw, black-edged hole just above her breast where a bullet had stabbed into her.

He lowered her head to the floor and pushed past Oconto and Kahena and Atahulla to take a look at Tahchee. A knife had been driven deep into his chest and blood darkened the floor around him. His lips were blue and his body had begun to stiffen. Atahulla, his blood brother, had turned his back to the body and was chanting a prayer to the Great Spirit to accept Tahchee as his own and make his brother's arm swift to avenge him.

There were two other rooms in the little house, and Mallonee swept one of the guttering candles up from the mantel and raced through them, the light held high, calling to Melissa as he went. But she was gone. Her carpetbag was packed and closed and sitting at the side of the bed—she'd been ready to ride away with them, he thought hopelessly—and then Wilcox had come and found her alone, and now she was gone.

He went back into the living room and ordered Ocowee and Tahonkee outside to search for sign of her. But despair told him that the search was hopeless. The blizzard would long since have wiped out any tracks.

The Cherokees had lifted Tahchee's body away from the over-turned chair that had been beneath it and Oconto had gone into the bedroom and come out with an eiderdown quilt of bright blue and red and yellow patches. They wrapped him in it as Mallonee watched and the chanting of their savage prayers was like the low throbbing of furious, deadly drums. There'd be no mercy for the man who'd killed Tahchee when they found him.

He crossed the room to the fireplace and locked his hands behind his back as he fought for steadiness and control.

One thing was plain enough to go ahead on—she'd been expecting Wilcox and his two guards that night. And they'd been there and done the double killing and kidnaped Melissa.

Mallonee's head came up at the sound of a horse's hoofs, coming down the little hill from the square and driving hard. He heard a man shout and a gun went off outside in the darkness, and then there was the sound of Ocowee and Tahonkee snarling and a man's voice cursing them in desperate frenzy. Mallonee jumped for the door and threw it open, peering out into the darkness. The two Cherokees were struggling with a man, only dimly seen. They were too much for him and in a final, shattering explosion of violence they forced him in through the door and slammed him hard against a wall.

He wasn't Wilcox. He was a stranger.

His cursing filled the room and his eyes were as wild as his efforts to break away from the two furious Indians. But there was no time to waste on him—no time to humor him or indulge him in his fury. Mallonee lashed out at the stranger's face with his open hand and the man's head slapped back from the blow and suddenly there was blood and the pattern of Mallonee's hand upon his face. In the instant of silence, Mallonee's fingers twisted into the other's scarf as he jerked the man forward.

"Shut off that damned racket, before I kill you! I want to know who you are—and why you're here."

The stranger's head came up; he looked at the tribesmen and then swung back to Mallonee again.

He said softly, "You're Mallonee, aren't you? You and these damned Indians of yours!"

He stared at Mallonee, and the beginning of a sardonic grin quivered and then died at the corners of his mouth. "We've met before. I fought with you—a little ruckus down at the state line about a week ago."

Mallonee checked himself, feeling the wild madness die a little in his brain. He'd had no chance to see the other in the fury of the fighting in the timber, but he knew now that this was the man who'd tried to club him to death with his gunbutt there at the last—the one Melissa had wounded, the only one who'd escaped alive.

"Then you're one of Wilcox's men," he said stonily, and his voice went flat and deadly as he took a quick step forward. "And you'll know what's happened here tonight and what's been done with Melissa." He whipped the razor-edged knife out of the knot in his belt and it came up with a whispering rush so that its point was tight against the stranger's throat. "Now talk, damn you—and talk straight and fast!"

But the stranger seemed to have gone on beyond any fear of Mallonee or anything that Mallonee could do. His body was still and his eyes were steady as the knife point went hard against his throat.

"I was one of Wilcox's men," he said steadily; "I'm not any more. I'm Jeffrey McCutcheon. Melissa is my wife!"

The words were like a clenched fist driven into Mallonee's face. He shook his head and let the knife drop back a little as he tried to fit them into the wild pattern of the night. He could see, looking at the stranger now, that he had the look about him of a man who had once been somebody, before his breeding had become blurred and distorted.

"She saw you when she shot at you," Mallonee said slowly. "But she didn't tell me who you were. She didn't say she knew you. She didn't say you were her husband."

"She didn't know me. It happened too fast; she didn't have a chance to see me. But I knew her—and that's why I sent word to Wilcox that you'd been killed. So she'd be safe from him when she came into Springfield."

"Safe!" The blood came up into Mallonee's face. "Does this look as if she was safe? Wilcox knew she'd been with me. He knew it the first night he was here—last night. He tried to make her tell him where I was. You didn't tell him that I was dead!"

The stranger's mouth twisted and the cold, black devils came back into his eyes. "I thought I did," he said harshly. "You've got a right to know, I guess. I dictated a note to Charlotte, but I found out tonight that she'd written another and told him the truth. That's why I'm here—but where is my wife? Mallonee, tell me what sort of a mess this damned play of yours has landed her in now?"

"I don't know. I don't know!" He let the knife slip back into its belt knot and motioned wearily to Ocowee and Tahonkee. "Let him loose. He's playing our game now—or he'd better be."

He watched the stranger jerk the cavalry jacket back up on his shoulders.

"All right, McCutcheon," he said grimly. "You want your wife—and I want her, too. And on top of that I want Wilcox. Wilcox and two men he'd hired as bodyguards were here tonight. They killed this woman and that Cherokee wrapped in the quilt. When we got here they had gone, and Melissa was gone with them. What do you know about that?"

"I know Dorsey Wilcox isn't going to live any longer than it takes me to get to him. I'll settle with you about Melissa after we find her."

He wasn't afraid to say what he meant, this Jeffrey McCutcheon, Mallonee admitted to himself. He'd been a good man once and he was still and probably dangerous.

"I've got five men with me—good men. We can handle Wilcox and his guards if we can get to them. But you can't. One man alone wouldn't have a chance. We've got to work together now. You figure out where he is, and we'll take care of him," Mallonee said.

"He won't keep her here in town," Jeff said slowly. "Too many people around to ask questions about what he's doing with her." He stroked his chin and his eyes seemed to look out past the walls of the room. "And he won't take her out to the farm—for he thinks I'm out there and he'd cut his own throat before he'd let us get together."

He swung away from the fireplace and began to pace up and down the room, completely oblivious of the men around him.

"He's got a couple of places south of here—an old timber camp down on the James that hasn't been working lately, and a farm on the Finley River. We can try the closer one first, and if they aren't there we'll go on to the other."

"We'll try it," Mallonee said tightly.

CHAPTER SEVENTEEN

THE WIND AND HAIL cut at Dorsey Wilcox's face while he held Melissa down against the ground in the ice-coated bushes that edged the curve of Jordan's Branch. The night was as black as a hole in hell and he began to realize what had happened. He'd killed a woman—his woman—in front of witnesses. He'd seen a man die once in this country for killing a woman—and his death hadn't been easy.

And the Cherokee Loosh had killed—he must have been one of Mallonee's men, and if he was there Mallonee wouldn't be far away. A steel band tightened around his throat as he realized that Mallonee and those damned red savages of his might be hunting him down while he crouched here.

There'd be a hell of a hue and cry, but unless Loosh and Arch came out against him, it would be hard to prove that he'd done it. And it came to him that there was a way to fix it so Loosh and Arch never could testify against him. Not tonight—for he needed them now—but later on, when the time was right. They were both professional gunmen and it wouldn't be easy, but he could find a time and a place to kill them without too much risk.

Now the big worry was Mallonee—Mallonee and those Indians. They'd kill him without thinking twice about it, that was sure. If he could find out where Mallonee was—if he could make this Melissa beside him break down and tell—there'd be a way to get him out of the way. And then, later, when he could get rid of Loosh and Arch, he'd be back where he started.

He turned to look down at the woman crouching on the ground beside him. She had the wool cloak wrapped tight around her, and she was staring straight ahead, her face expressionless except for a trembling that struck her now and then. She'd been like that ever since he'd dragged her out of the house. Frozen and empty-eyed and moving like a mechanical doll. It would be hard to make her talk, but there were ways to do it.

He heard horses trampling through the underbrush on the other side of the creek. He crouched down close to the ground and drew his gun and waited with the breath harsh and short in his throat.

"Dorsey! Dorsey, where in th' hell are you?" It was Loosh's voice, ugly with strain.

"Over here, Loosh."

He saw their shadows loom up as black forms in the rain and then Loosh's horse was splashing across the swollen stream and Loosh was pulling at the reins of two horses that followed him.

Between them, they picked up the woman and dumped her down into the saddle. Dorsey gagged her with his handkerchief, untied the stake rope, and lashed it from one of her ankles to the other, passing it under the horse's belly and pulling it up tight so there'd be no chance for her to get away. With the gag and the rope she couldn't call for help, and she couldn't jump and run. He had her now.

They struck south out of town toward the James River, staying away from the roads and riding through the fields and the timber, swinging wide whenever they came to a farmhouse or a cabin in a clearing. His timber camp was half a mile below McKinley Ford and back in the woods and if they reached it they wouldn't be bothered no matter what they had to do.

It was slow going, with the wind and the rain and the sleet and the irregular course that they had to follow, and it was close to midnight when they hit the log road and turned east toward the timber camp. They were almost level with the bunkhouse and he was beginning to breathe easier when a dog ran out at him and another one joined him and he suddenly realized that there were two canvas-covered wagons—settlers' wagons, immigrant wagons—drawn up beside the building. The dogs came closer and began to bark and run at the horses.

It turned him sick inside, for he'd been counting on this place, and if some movers had got caught here by the storm and moved in, it was going to ruin everything he'd planned. He grabbed the bridle of Melissa's horse and pulled both horses back around the corner of the bunkhouse, where they'd be out of sight. A light had flared up inside the building, and he didn't want some fool to find him guarding a gagged and hogtied woman. Loosh came trotting up and he kneed his horse in against him so they could talk without being overheard.

"Loosh," he said sharply, "you get over there and find out who's camped here and get them out of here. No matter who they are or what they say—get them out of here!"

Loosh looked at Wilcox with a jeering twist to his mouth. He said contemptuously, "Suppose there's women an' children in there. You want me to pitch 'em out into this storm in the middle of the night?"

"I don't give a damn what you do," Wilcox snapped. "We've got to have that place and we've got to have it tonight. Now get on over there."

"I'll take a look at it," Loosh said noncommittally. He pulled his horse around and rode over to face the doorway.

"Who's in there?" he yelled. "What's goin' on in there? Show yourself!"

The door came open and a bony-shouldered man with a double-barreled shotgun in his hands came out on to the doorstep.

"We're camped here," he said, and his voice was mournful. "We come from Arkansas, an' we're headin' for Kansas to take up a homestead. You got any objections to us usin' this place?"

"You'll have to get out." Loosh's voice was mean, as if he didn't like the job Wilcox had given him. "Pack up your stuff an' haul outa here. This ain't a public campin' ground."

"The hell it ain't!" The man moved back a little and the gun-barrel shifted until it was pointed straight at Loosh's belly. "Well, I'm goin' to tell you somethin', mister. My wife's havin' a baby in there right now, an' if you think we're goin' to pack up and move with her in thet shape then you ain't got any brains. I got this gun, an' I got three brothers an' two grown boys with me—an' they all got guns. You figure you're man enough to throw us out of here, start gettin' at it!"

He glared at Loosh, and then the door slammed shut and Wilcox heard a bar go down across it. Loosh gathered up his reins and came riding back.

"You heard him," he said flatly. "If you want him out of there, you go right ahead an' get him out. But it ain't a job for Arch or me."

And it wasn't any job for Wilcox, either. Desperate as he was, he knew that the bony-shouldered man held all the aces.

He picked up the reins of his horse and Melissa's and turned out toward the log road again. Out there, without the shelter of the trees, the sleet bit at them like whips. He turned upstream toward McKinley's Ford. He knew now that they were going to have to cross the stream and go south for another ten miles, until they came to a piece of land down on the Finley where there was a dilapidated old house sitting on an eighty-foot cliff that over-looked the river. It was a hell of a place, but it would have to do for tonight.

CHAPTER EIGHTEEN

LATER, REMEMBERING IT, Melissa knew that she'd been like a dead woman on that awful ride from Springfield to the house on the cliff over the river. There was a nightmare quality to it all—a nightmare of trying desperately to break out of a ring of horror that kept closing in around her. And yet all the time she couldn't move and she couldn't speak and her mind was full of despair.

Their horses fought their way up a steep ridge of rock and fine shale that slipped and turned under their hoofs. Suddenly they came out on top of a flat, wind-whipped ledge of stone that was bare of trees and ended abruptly in a sheer cliff that plunged down to a foaming, white crested river far below. It was long past midnight.

When Wilcox jerked at her horse's reins and the jarring, endless movement stopped, it had no meaning for her. Hours before, she'd lost all sense of significance in what they were doing. Her world had shrunk into a tight little circle that contained nothing except her aching body and a filthy gag that choked her when she tried to breathe and a tight-pulled rope that had long since rubbed the flesh away from her ankles so that now they were raw and tender and burned like fire.

Dully, she watched the three men climb down from their saddles and realized that Wilcox and Loosh were working at the knots that held the rope. They jerked at them impatiently, and the rough Manila sawed and cut at her flesh again. Then the rope fell away and Wilcox jerked at her arm, pulling her down out of the saddle. She tried to swing free, but she was too stiff with cold and came plunging awkwardly down, almost head first, and would have smashed into the ground if Wilcox had not caught her and swung her back up on her feet again. She tried to take a step and stumbled and almost fell, for the circulation had stopped in her feet and legs.

She tried again, and this time she did fall, with a thousand knives and needles shooting up through her legs in an exquisite torture. He swore again and jerked her up off the ground and shook her like a dog shaking a rat.

"You're no worse off than the rest of us," he said brutally. "Just stand there a minute while we get these saddles stripped off and you'll be able to make it all right."

As the men worked with the horses, she clung to a sapling that had pushed its way up through the rock. Her head was swimming, pain in her legs and feet was sharp and pitiless.

Through the veils of sleet that slashed down like furious lances falling, she could make out the low bulk of a building, almost at the edge of the cliff. Loosh and Arch had picketed the horses where they'd have the shelter of the timber that edged up to the barren rock, and now they shouldered the four saddles and went stumbling away toward the house while Wilcox came back to her. His hand closed down around her arm, just above the elbow, and he jerked her away from the sapling that she'd been using as a crutch.

"Come on," he growled impatiently. "Let's get in out of this damn weather and find a fire before we freeze to death."

He pulled her along beside him, until the hulk of the building loomed up before them. He pushed her through a door and she saw Loosh on his knees in front of a fireplace, striking a flame and feeding it into a pile of firewood inside the wide cavern of the hearth. Arch was carrying more wood from some shed at the back and as the flames leaped up she saw that the room they were in was small and low-ceilinged, built of rough logs and empty of furniture except for a rough table and a broken, straight-backed chair. The clay that had chinked the crevices between the logs had hardened and fallen away so that sleet drove in through the gaps and lay in white and uneven windrows across the floor.

The fire began to spread and brighten, and she started toward it, numb and miserable and wooden-legged, as if it had been a magnet drawing her. Loosh looked at her, wolf-eyed, and then moved a little to one side as she went down on her knees on the hearth stone, holding out her hands to the heat and pushing her wet cloak back on her shoulders so the warmth could reach her body. She heard him grunt and knew that he had turned to see her better, and she remembered, dully and without caring, that she was naked above the waist, just as she had been ever since the red-haired vixen had ripped her bodice away in the cabin so many hours before.

She should have tried to cover herself, the nightmare of the night had stripped the veneer away and left her with nothing except a dull instinct for survival. Her body was nothing but a penance and a punishment that would not let her rest.

The saddles had been dumped in a corner of the room, and she watched dully as Arch bent over them, picking them up and shifting them, bringing up one saddlebag after another and searching through them, until suddenly she heard a growl of satisfaction. He came striding across to the fire with a quart bottle in his hand.

"I figured this ought to come in right good when I seen it on a rafter down at the livery stable." He worked the cork out of the neck with a knife blade and tipped it up to his mouth and held it there until she thought he meant to drain the bottle. Finally he brought it down, and held the bottle out to Loosh.

"Ain't nothin' like it," he said huskily. "Good whisky'll put a man on his horse an' drive a woman outa her petticoats." He looked at her and his mouth twisted into a hard grin and his eyes raked her as hungrily as if they had been hands clawing at her.

"Most especially when she ain't got nothin' but her petticoats on to start with."

His words cracked the shell of stunned insensibility that had been like a coating of ice upon her. She jerked her head around to stare at him, and there was no mistaking the look on his face. Battered and beaten and frozen or not, she was still a woman and he meant to use her as one before he was done.

She squeezed her eyes tight shut and jerked the cloak tight around her and tried to turn away from him, but the booming sound of his laughter hammered at her and would not let her escape.

The firelight flicked against her eyelids and she opened her eyes. Wilcox had the bottle now and he was coughing and choking as he lowered it from his lips. He shook his head and blew breath quickly out of his mouth. He said, gasping, "Great God, what that'll do to a man!"

He looked at her, and his eyes hesitated, shifted, and then came back to her again. He weighed the bottle speculatively in his hand and then he took a quick step forward and held it out to her.

"Here," he said roughly. "Get some of this inside of you and see if you can't smarten up a little. You look to me like you was half froze. You won't be any good to us if you're dead."

"Wouldn't be near as much good, would she, Dorsey?" Arch roared with laughter and dug his elbow into Wilcox's ribs.

"She's not going to cash out on us," Wilcox said flatly. "She's going to take that drink and get her tongue to working again and then she's going to tell me every thing that she knows about Mallonee."

"To hell with that, Dorsey." Arch's voice cracked like a whip. "You an' her can set an' talk about Mallonee till your tongues drop out far as I'm concerned—but first things got to come first." He swung around to her and his eyes were hot and furious and intent.

"Take your drink, woman," he said roughly. "An' take a damn good one, because you're goin' to need it."

She tried to speak, to move, but this horror growing before her eyes held her. She tried to get to her feet, with some wild idea of escaping them and running out into the freezing night again, but she couldn't stir. She was abjectly afraid, and as her head went down and a spasm of shuddering tore at her, she realized that she still had the bottle in her hand. There was no cork in it and the rank fumes of the whisky burned in her nostrils and she knew, sharply and objectively, that no matter what was to come the alcohol would make it easier to bear. The harsh fire of it burned her throat and she gasped and held it there and gulped it down until Loosh swore angrily and bent over and jerked it away from her.

She could feel it biting into her now, clear down her throat and into her stomach and swirling like fire in her brain. The icy shell that had held her seemed to break and shatter and there was a tingling that went all through her body. She was still afraid, but the blind, senseless panic was gone. She could look at them now and see them as three roughly dressed, hard-faced men rather than as implacable devils straight out of hell.

She got to her feet. She couldn't fight them with her bare hands—but she could fight them in a woman's way, with the things she could say to them and the jealousies she could stir up between them.

"Dorsey," she said pleadingly, and she turned to him and held his eyes with hers, "you know you didn't have to bring me here to find out what you wanted—or get what you wanted. I promised you that last night, when you were at the cottage." He frowned and a low growl gathered in his throat, but she rushed on before he could remember too much. "But this other man—" she shot a quick glance at Arch and let her lip curl scornfully—"if you're a man, I don't think you're going to let him have me!"

It was a challenge, and she knew that events had driven him into so desperate a corner that he didn't dare let them snatch the leadership and the dominance away from him. His only hope now was to drive them down the road he had to go. If he knuckled under to them once, they'd be tyrants instead of supporters— and he'd have no allies at all to help him fight off the pressing threat of Mallonee's fury.

He glared at her, with his teeth gnawing at his lower lip, and the hot flush the whisky had given him draining out of his face. His thoughts had followed hers, but the cowardice inside held him back and pleaded for some compromise short of violence. He jerked his shoulders uneasily, raised one hand, and brought it down on Arch's shoulder in a gesture of comradely understanding.

"Why, hell," he said, and he tried hard to make his voice sure and easy and masculine, "Arch wasn't going to do anything to you. He was just carrying you along with that kind of talk so he could laugh at you. He didn't mean—"

"Don't try to tell me what I meant, Dorsey!"

Arch's face had hardened into a snarl and he raised his arm and struck Dorsey's hand away.

"She heard what I said plain enough, and so did you!" His arm shot out and his fingers dug into her shoulder. He snarled, "Come here to me!"

But she'd seen the desperation growing in Wilcox's face and seen the muscles tighten in his throat in the instant before his hand went streaking down toward his gun. Arch caught it, too, and his free arm plunged toward his holster. But she whirled and threw her arms around him so that he couldn't pull the gun free. Then she heard Loosh's voice half a dozen feet away, as cold and as uncompromising as the crack of doom.

"Both of you drop them guns and stand steady, unless you want a bullet into your guts. I've had enough of this damn foolishness, an' I've got a hide to save even if the rest of you ain't.

Turn the woman loose an' step back, Arch. Dorsey—you make one move an' I'll kill you!"

The silence was like the throbbing vacuum that comes on the heels of a clap of thunder. And then she felt Arch relax and his hand fell away from her and she stepped back and turned to look at Loosh and saw his face twist.

"You've both forgot what happened back in Springfield last night!" His voice was cold. "I don't know too much yet about this Mallonee Dorsey's dodging, but I've kept my ears open an' my mouth shut. It's plain to me that the Injun I killed back there was one of his men, an' there's plenty more where he come from. I figure Dorsey's got big trouble gunnin' for him, and thet means it's gunnin' for us, too. If this little biddy can tell us where it is, the thing for us to do is get her talkin' and do it right now. Maybe there'll be time to pleasure ourselves after that's done, but like you said a while ago, Arch, first things got to come first."

Her heart seemed to sicken and die inside her, for Loosh had driven straight to the heart of the problem. They'd ask questions that had to be answered, and if she told them the truth Mallonee was doomed and so was she. And if she lied to them—

Arch growled deep in his throat, but there was a look of relief growing in Wilcox's face as he stared at Loosh. He'd been forced into a position that he'd hated and dreaded, but now this reprieve had freed him from the obligation that Melissa had thrust upon him. He turned his head slowly to look at her, and she realized that his resentment was being transferred to her. There'd be no forgiveness in his heart for what she'd almost done to him.

"You've got it right, Loosh," he said decisively. "And I'll tell you this about Mallonee. He's hard and dangerous, and he's got those Cherokees with him. If he catches up with us, it's going to be bad. But this woman knows where he is. She knows what sort of plans he's made. Once we find out about them from her we'll have the whip hand again."

Arch moved in on her with a rush and his fingers dug in like claws, into the soft, tender skin just below her breast.

"Start talkin', damn you!" he growled. The fingers went in a little deeper and pain hit her. "Where is this Mallonee?

"I don't know!" she cried. "I don't know where he. is! I wish I did know!"

"That's a damn lie!"

Wilcox had come up behind her. "You left him waiting somewhere while you came in on the stage and tried to find out what he'd be sticking his neck into if he came into Springfield himself. That's the way of it, isn't it? That's just what you did!"

"I was there when Jeff tried to kill us," she gasped. "And Mallonee was hurt—badly hurt." She realized that she'd started to babble and checked her words and tried desperately to think of some explanation she could give them that they'd believe.

"Let's hear the rest of it."

"But that's all there is!" She was clinging to Arch's arm to hold herself erect and the tears were pouring down her cheeks. "A party of movers came by in two wagons the next day. They were going from Ft. Smith to St. Louis—and I left Mallonee there with his Indians and went along with them."

"How come you rode into Springfield on the Rolla stage if you'd started to St. Louis with these movers?"

"I didn't stay with them. When we got to the road where the stage line ran, I caught the stage and came into Springfield. I wanted to find my husband—I still want to. I don't know anything about your trouble with Mallonee, and I don't want to know!"

She saw Loosh turn to look at Wilcox and shove out his lower lip in a grimace of doubt and inquiry.

"How does thet sound to you, Dorsey?" he asked skeptically. "You figger it hooks up with the things that have happened since she come in to Springfield on the stage the other day?"

"What about that Indian last night?" Wilcox demanded. "There's not a damned Cherokee within two hundred miles of here except the ones Mallonee brought up from Mississippi. Don't try to tell me that wasn't one of Mallonee's men."

"Mallonee sent him to me," she said. "From down in Arkansas, where he and Jeffrey had the fight. He said Mallonee wasn't able to travel, and he wanted me to come to him."

"He didn't say Mallonee was comin' to you, did he?" Loosh cut in harshly.

"Oh, no," she sobbed. "He couldn't. I just told you he couldn't travel."

"That's what you said." Loosh's disbelief was open and undisguised. "I figure she's lying faster'n a horse can trot, Dorsey."

Wilcox's voice pounded at her like a sledge. "Mallonee—Mallonee—" It seemed that his voice was going farther and farther away. "Mallonee—where's Mallonee?"

She was falling forward when she heard a chorus of savage voices screaming like demons somewhere outside the walls, and half a dozen pistol shots slammed into the log walls of the house. Abruptly, she was free from the iron hands that had held her. In the same instant she saw the three men scatter as they dived for the dark corners of the room.

The shouts came again, piercing and blood-chilling, and Melissa knew they were Mallonee's Cherokees. A voice that had the sound of a snarling trumpet was shouting orders, and gunfire hammered against the house again. A gun answered them, not ten feet away to her left, and a scream of pain answered it. She jerked her head around and saw that Loosh was prone on the floor, his belt gun in his hand, firing coolly out into the darkness through a crack between the logs where the clay chinking had fallen away.

His face was stony, intense, frozen into the hard mask of killing. He raised the gun again, sighting along its barrel as deliberately as if he had been in a shooting gallery. The gun cracked and jumped and she heard another scream outside. Two men down already; two men—and perhaps one of them Mallonee—victims of this grim-faced demon who was dealing death from behind the shelter of the cabin walls.

Her eyes searched for a weapon, and she saw a stick of wood as thick through as her arm that had fallen out upon the hearth, one end of it still blazing but the other untouched by the fire. She had it and threw it in a single motion, straight at his face. It whirled like a knife and struck him square in the temple. He roared like a bull and threw himself to one side, clawing and beating at the torch, his gun forgotten on the floor beside him. She gathered herself and dived for it, but he saw her coming and his boot lashed out and caught her in the shoulder, slamming her back against the cabin wall and making her feel faint.

He threw himself forward and grabbed the gun. It went up and came down in a vicious blow as she tried to get away from it. Her head seemed to split open as if an axe had been driven into it, and a whirlpool of dizzying light shattered in her brain.

The room and the thundering of the gunfire seemed to fade away. Dimly, like some spectator watching from a long way off, she realized that Arch was dragging her across the floor. He pulled her through a narrow doorway into a dark, slant-roofed room—the room at the back of the cabin, she thought vaguely, where he'd got the wood to build the fire. He suddenly let her go and she fell to the floor.

Then he was gone, and the narrow door closed behind him, and she heard the sound of a bar being forced into place to lock it shut.

CHAPTER NINETEEN

I T WAS AN HOUR PAST MIDNIGHT when they came to the timber camp Jeff had indicated as a possible hiding place for Wilcox. He and Mallonee were in the lead, with Atahulla and Oconto close behind them, while Tahonkee and Kahena and Ocowee brought up the rear. There was a flicker of light from the bunkhouse windows and Jeff leaned forward and slapped his hand down hard on his thigh.

"By hell!" he said tensely. "We've caught him!"

Mallonee grunted doubtfully and checked his horse.

"I hope you're right." The long-held suspense and the deadly fury inside him had turned his voice cold and savage. "But what about those movers' wagons shoved up there by the door? He didn't take time to bring her down here in any damned wagon."

A chorus of barking dogs cut off his words, and two hounds came charging up out of the shadows by the door. The horses danced and jerked away in sudden alarm and the clamor of the hounds increased as they raced in, snarling and nipping at the horses' heels.

"They'll know we're here now," Mallonee said grimly. He leaned down and forward and the end of his riding quirt caught one of the hounds across the shoulders and sent him back toward the shelter of the house, yelping and crying. The bunkhouse door slammed open and the figures of two men carrying long-barreled guns slipped through the light and into the darkness outside. The door slammed shut behind them and Mallonee clawed the hand gun out of his holster and spun his horse to one side as he tried to see into the shadows where they had disappeared.

A man's rough-edged voice hailed them from the blackness against the house. "I told you once we wasn't gettin' out of here tonight! Now, damn you, get out an' stay out or you're goin' to get a double charge of buckshot. I won't warn you again!"

"Why, God damn you—"

Jeff had his gun out and up in the split second before Mallonee's voice checked him.

"Hold it, all of you! That's not Wilcox—and we haven't been here before."

He raised his voice, projecting it through the darkness to the hidden gunmen beside the door.

"Whoever you are, listen to me a minute." His voice had a hard precision. "We haven't been here before. You didn't warn us away. We're looking for three men and a woman, and we think they came by here—maybe they're here now. Have you seen them?"

"Hell no. There was a couple of overbearin' sons here an hour or more ago that talked big at first an' sung small at the last. But they tucked their tails an' left when I let 'em know I didn't want no argument outa 'em."

"And they didn't have a woman with them? You're sure about that?"

"I didn't say they didn't have no woman. Might of had a whole passel of 'em forty feet away an' I couldn't have seen 'em with the sleet an' rain. I didn't see no woman. If they had one with 'em, I didn't know nothin' about it."

"Which way did they go?"

"Went back down the road towards the river, far as I could see."

"Well—" Mallonee's voice was harsh in the darkness, "that's that, then. Let's head for the Finley River, Jeff."

They turned the horses on the light crust that was forming on the ground, the slivers of ice snapping and crackling like fire beneath the horses' hoofs.

"You go back toward the river to get to this other place, McCutcheon?"

"Ford the James, and then ten miles off to the south and east." Jeff's voice was surly with disappointment. "You think that was Wilcox that stopped back there—and he had Melissa hid out somewhere?"

"It sounds like it. There wouldn't be too many travelers out on a night like this."

It seemed that the going was worse after they had forded the James, for the rutted excuse for a road that they'd been following turned away to the west and they came into a stretch of country that was torn and serried by sharp hills and deep-plunging valleys. The Cherokees grew more restive with every mile that passed. Every man among them felt that the death of Tahchee was an outrage that must be erased in blood. For Atahulla, Tahchee's blood brother, the waiting and searching were almost beyond bearing.

The cavalcade clattered down a long hill, and at its bottom Jeff waved his arm toward an almost vertical slope ahead of them.

"Up there," he said, "we'll find an old cabin. And I think we'll find Wilcox, too."

The Cherokees, riding close at his heels, caught the words above the howling fury of the wind-whipped storm. Mallonee saw them exchange glances and as he put his horse to the slope, he saw that they had fanned out into a sort of skirmish line so that now they rode alongside of him instead of behind him. It was a difficult advance, for the sleet had coated the slope with ice and the horses' hoofs could hardly dig through it. Almost at the top, Mallonee's horse lost its footing and he had to swing down out of the saddle while it scrambled to its feet again. In the moment he went down, the Cherokees went ahead of him, and as he clambered back into the saddle, he heard their blood-chilling war cry. Gunfire hammered at the night and he swore and pushed his horse forward until he could see a lonely cabin outlined against the sky, with great lines of light coming through the unfilled cracks between its logs.

Ocowee was already unhorsed and sprawled not a dozen feet from the cabin doorway, his gun twenty feet away where it had fallen when the bullet that was his death came from the cabin. Mallonee saw the flash of a gun inside the cabin, far down, almost at the floor, and jerked his head around just in time to see Kahena throw up his hands and go plunging down out of the saddle. The three other Cherokees had checked their first charge, confounded by the unexpected resistance from the cabin. Jeff had drawn rein in the shelter of the trees. Mallonee swore in impatient fury and his voice went up in a command.

"Get back into the trees! Get back, damn it! Back here where I am—"

Battle-trained, the three tribesmen swung low on their horses' necks and whirled their mounts. Heels hammering hard, they brought the panting horses in under the trees at a dead gallop, and were out of their saddles and turned back toward the cabin while Mallonee's shout was still ringing in the air.

"Surround the damned place—" Mallonee's voice bit at them. "If they're in there, we don't want them to get away. Jeff, you and Oconto get off to the right, towards that cliff there. Atahulla, you and Tahonkee cover the left. Jump now, before they break out of some back door and skip out on us."

They scattered like shadows. Jeff disappeared around the house to the right and the three Indians merged into the darkness and dropped out of sight as abruptly as if a giant mouth had swallowed them. From the scanty shelter of the naked trees, Mallonee surveyed the cabin, racking his brain for some stratagem that would insure Melissa's safety and the taking of Wilcox alive, without sacrificing more of his men.

The cabin was a small structure, not more than one room, he judged, although there might be a lean-to shed connected at the back for the storage of dry wood and kindling. A flickering light danced and burned inside the main room, revealed through the wide cracks between the logs in the cabin walls.

His jaw hardened as he faced the fact that there was only one way to do it in the time they had—a frontal assault on the door with gunmen behind them to push the defenders back from the walls while they made a run for it. It was a long chance, a desperate gamble—but it was that or nothing.

He whistled softly and after a moment the three Cherokees were back beside him, their faces hard and ominous, their bodies tensed for instant action.

"We'll have to rush them," he said grimly, and heard Atahulla's quick indrawn breath of satisfaction. "Oconto, you and Tahonkee swing out on either side of the door and start pouring lead in between those cracks so fast that those bastards inside won't know what hit them. Atahulla and I will try to crash the door. Once it's open, and we're inside, come on in after us like the very devil was after you."

"The other man—McCutcheon?" Oconto's voice was stiff with doubt.

"He's around at the back. We'll leave him there." There wasn't any use in reminding them that Jeff had been Wilcox's man before and he might be yet, as ready to change colors now as he had been in Melissa's cottage. To hell with him, Mallonee thought savagely. He'd deal with him when this was out of the way.

The four of them moved out across the icy ground toward the black panel of the door. Oconto and Tahonkee fell back a little, and as Mallonee and Atahulla ran forward they heard the sudden volleying of shots rise behind them.

Mallonee's shoulder struck the door like a battering ram and as the time-rotted latch snapped the door slammed open. It was hard to see the room clearly at first, for the firelight blinded him and the shadows were distorted and confusing. Dimly he made out two men against the opposite wall, and he snapped a shot at the nearest one just as Atahulla lunged through the door behind him. The man he had fired on clutched at his shoulder, spun in a half circle and went down, but the other had his gun up and as fire blazed from its muzzle he heard Atahulla groan as if a two-by-four had been driven into his belly. He turned and saw the Cherokee clutching at the wall, his face frozen agony and his legs crumpling beneath him.

He whirled back to fire at the man who had killed Atahulla, but shooting in the dancing light was like shooting into a distorted mirror, and the shot went wild. The door, blown half closed, slammed open again, and Tahonkee came through it with the gun barking in his hand and Oconto just behind him. The gunman against the wall fired twice, two shots so close together that one seemed the echo of the other, and Tahonkee reeled and staggered forward two more stumbling steps before he went down, his arms still reaching toward the man who had murdered him.

Back of Mallonee, in the corner hidden by the door and almost untouched by the light of the fire, a gun exploded savagely and Mallonee turned to see Wilcox, bent-legged and white-faced, crouching in the corner with his gun raised for another shot. The gun in Mallonee's hand came up like a striking serpent and then, in the second that his finger tightened on the trigger, he remembered that he must try to take Wilcox alive, and the muzzle shifted toward Wilcox's shoulder. But the afterthought had come too fast to allow accurate shooting, and the bullet shaved Wilcox's arm and buried itself in the log wall behind him.

Oconto had driven straight for Loosh; Loosh had dodged and fired, and Oconto's rush had carried him headlong into the wall, the blood streaming out of his mouth as he fell.

Loosh lifted the gun to fire again, but the hammer clicked on an empty chamber and he swore and whirled around to face the door again.

Mallonee and Wilcox were in a tangle on the floor, both their guns lost in the darkness. They rolled over and over, kicking and gouging each other, their hands tearing at each other's throats.

Loosh swore at the empty gun in his hand and then he flipped it into the air, reversing it so that the barrel was clenched in his fist and the heavy butt became a deadly hammer. He plunged toward Mallonee with the gun raising in a savage arc.

The exposed cliff top at the back of the house was a place of freezing torture, Jeff had discovered when he'd taken up the position Mallonee had assigned him. Wind and blinding hail swept across the wide valley to the east and hurdled the river and flung itself at the emptiness of the barren cliff like a savage army storming a castle turret. It bit into his bones and tightened around his lungs with icy fingers. No man could endure it. He looked around him for shelter, and the box like lean-to jutting out from the back of the cabin suggested itself as a windbreak. He hunched his shoulders and fought his way across the icy ground to it, his feet slipping and sliding beneath him, his arms waving as he tried to maintain his balance against the wind and ice.

It was better in the lee of the shed. The wind howled past and the sleet was a white and fiercely driving curtain, but they could not reach him there. He grunted in sour satisfaction and began to examine the wall of the shed that sheltered him. It had a two-foot-square window, covered by a heavy plank shutter that was held tight against the wall by a slanting pole that had one end braced against a nearby stump and the other hard against the window. He stared at it, too numbed by the cold at first to realize that this might provide another entrance into the cabin, an unguarded entrance that would, if it could be breached, allow him to take the defenders in the rear. A roar of shouts and gun-fire erupted in the main room of the cabin and he realized that the fight had shifted to the inside of the building. They had gone in without him; the realization lashed at him like a whip, and he began to hammer at the pole that braced the shutter closed.

It was frozen under a coating of ice, but he threw his weight against it, knocking it aside. Then he jerked it up from the ground again and used its point as a lever to pry the shutter free. There was no glass, no parchment, behind it; nothing except a yawn-ing blackness and an emptiness and—he lifted hs head unbeliev-ingly—the muffled sound of a woman sobbing and beating her fists against a door.

"Melissa!" His voice was incredulous. "Melissa! Are you in there? Melissa—answer me!"

The sobbing and the pounding stopped as abruptly as if she had been frozen in a paralyzed balance of fear and hope.

"Who is it?" Her voice was shaken, hardly audible. "Oh, Mallonee! Darling, I've prayed for you to come—"

It seemed to Jeff that all the blood in his body was suddenly drained away. Mallonee, he thought fiercely. He's the one she wants—not me! He took a deep breath, and his voice was bitter as he answered her.

"Not Mallonee—no. Your luck's not that good. This is your husband, the man you forgot about."

He could hear her quick gasp of surprise, and then her hands were groping for him in the darkness.

"Oh, Jeff—Jeff—" she sobbed. "Are you with them, or with Wilcox?"

"With them? With your lover, you mean? With Mallonee?"

"Oh, Jeff," her voice trailed away into anguish. "You aren't with Wilcox. You couldn't be!"

"I'm not with Wilcox. I'm through with him. But I didn't come here to help Mallonee, either. I came here to get you and get out."

"Oh, no! I couldn't leave him like that. You'll have to help, Jeff. Loosh and Wilcox are killing him—I saw them through a crack in the door! You've got to help him, Jeff! You can break the door down and then go in and—"

Unseen in the darkness, his mouth twisted in sardonic amusement. So this was to be his role—to be the defender and the saviour of his wife's lover. The word was as bitter as all the lost promise of his youth, all the pretences and the self-deceits and the shabby compromises that had been his. For an instant he had a quixotic impulse to toss this last shred of himself into the cauldron with the rest—then it was gone and he was himself again, Jeffrey McCutcheon, loyal to nothing and to no one beyond his own hungers and desires.

"I'll come inside," he said shortly. "Then we'll see about it."

He put his palms on the window ledge and eased himself into the blank darkness in front of him. The window frame scraped his shoulder and threw him sideways and his left wrist buckled and snapped beneath his weight as he struck a rough-edged pile of wood and timber. The pain cut at him like a knife, but he found his feet, feeling for Melissa with his uninjured hand. His fingers touched her and she cried out like a frightened child. He put his arm around her and she came to him, trembling, her face wet with tears.

"Melissa—" he said, and it seemed to him that the very name tore at his throat. "We can start out all over again. We can get out of this terrible place—go out to Oregon—"

She didn't answer, and the bitterness of her implied rejection turned the brief tenderness he had felt into a rough-scaled anger. Abruptly, he knew that he would take her and keep her by any means he could grasp. Once Mallonee was dead she'd come back to her senses, back to the desires and the common need they'd once shared. He could feel determination hardening within him, and a recklessness that counted every man his enemy, that asked no quarter and that granted none.

"Where's the door?" he said grimly.

He swung away from her and plunged at the door, his left shoulder driving into it and the shock sending lances of pain down into his broken wrist. The door swayed, held, and he lunged against it again. The light pole that was its bar on the other side cracked and splintered away. He was through it and out into the other room with his pistol coming up out of its holster as Loosh's gun swept down toward Mallonee's head. The gun jumped in his hand and Loosh's body stiffened, staggered to one side as if a giant hand had struck him, and went crashing down across the floor.

Jeff's eyes jerked around to the snarled figures of Wilcox and Mallonee, trapped in the life-and-death struggle that engulfed them. They moved so swiftly that there was no chance of a fair shot. He moved in on them, gun balanced and ready, his eyes so intent upon them that he did not see the faint stir of movement across the room as Arch, his blind urge toward survival still flickering above the mortal hurt Mallonee's pistol shot had given him, saw Loosh go down. For Arch, the lesson was plain enough; he clawed on the floor for his own gun, raised it in a quivering hand, and sent a bullet plowing straight into Jeffrey's back.

It seemed to Jeffrey that a black fog billowed up around him as he turned slowly, his eyes half glazed and his body swaying, as he searched the shadowy room for the source of this new attack. He could see Arch now, half raised on an arm that was already buckling beneath him, the pistol drooping as his fingers relaxed their grip. The fog rolled higher, and in the instant before it engulfed him Jeff's finger hardened around the trigger and the gun sent its bullet smashing into Arch's forehead, just above his staring eyes.

Wilcox had seen Jeff burst into the room and Loosh go down, and glimpsed the final drama of Jeff's and Arch's deaths. He was all alone now—the blind terror of the thought galvanized him into a final, desperate savagery. He jerked himself free and his boot crashed into Mallonee's stomach, slamming him backward and bending him double in agony. It was a reprieve, and on the instant Wilcox was across the room and out the door, slipping and sliding and trying to run toward the shelter of the trees where the horses were tethered.

But Kahena was waiting to turn him back. His shoulder splintered by a bullet and his right leg crushed where his horse had fallen upon him, Kahena was still too much the warrior to concede that his share of the fighting was done. His bullet lashed out at Wilcox when the fugitive was no more than a dozen feet outside the door. It missed him, but it was enough to turn him back around the corner of the cabin, back toward the ice-coated slope that slanted sharply downward toward the sheer drop of the cliff. He was running in blind terror now, without hope or purpose or direction.

The icy ground was as treacherous as oiled glass, and he was almost over the edge and down the frozen lip that edged the cliff before he caught himself and clawed his way back to safety. A hoarse voice roared at him, and he saw Mallonee round the corner of the cabin and come at him in a rush. He screamed and tried to run again. Then Mallonee was on him, hands clawing at his throat, fists battering him, pushing him back.

He tried to fight back, blindly and helplessly. His flailing arm struck the low-hanging branch of a half-grown elm tree just at the edge of the slope. His fingers locked around it in a frantic convulsion and he swung sideways, kicked out, and gasped in incredulous relief as he felt his boots crash into Mallonee's ankles and sweep his legs out from under him. Mallonee went down, his body spinning on the ice-sheathed ground, and in an instant Wilcox was plunging toward him. A moment ago it had seemed hopeless, but now a quick thrust of the foot, a kick in the face, would send Mallonee spinning down into the great emptiness below and Wilcox would be completely safe again.

For Mallonee, it was a nightmare, a furious, deadly madness of desperation, this clawing for a finger hold on the icy edge of a precipice. He was half off the edge when his fingers closed around a twisted, half-buried root. He jerked his head around and saw Wilcox coming in for the kill. Half bent, running, his aim was plain enough.

Mallonee spun and rolled, bringing himself up into a half-sitting position. His leg lashed out at Wilcox in the same split heartbeat of time that Wilcox's boot came swinging in. For a moment they were tangled together, and then Mallonee's heel came down in a terrible, down-thrashing blow and Wilcox staggered back, his own leg half paralyzed and his arms flailing wildly about in the air.

Mallonee gathered himself for a final effort and lunged forward. He felt Wilcox going backward, staggering, falling, and then Wilcox's knee came up in a shattering explosion that caught him just below the chin and across the throat.

A torrent of orange light seemed to explode in Mallonee's brain. He realized, dimly, that Wilcox was still erect and coming toward him now, the heavy boots moving closer and closer. He couldn't fight back this time; he couldn't roll away. Helpless, he saw one of the boots coming up from the ground, lifting, rising, swinging in the deadly arc—

A gun cracked, somewhere far away and at the same time intimately close to him. It had no meaning, no significance. There was nothing real except the brutally swinging boot.

The gun cracked again just as the boot came down. He felt his head jarred, knocked aside, and waited for the pain of the blow. But it did not come. The boot had scraped him, almost missed him. Through the blaze of orange light, he saw Wilcox's body immense above him, swaying, turning—and then its dead weight suddenly falling upon him so that his chest seemed to collapse and there was a sudden, cramping sickness, and then nothing else at all.

He came back to consciousness with his head cradled in Melissa's lap and the feel of her hands scrubbing snow and sleet into his cheeks and temples. He was cold; the night seemed to surround him and encase him in freezing sheets of icy wind. He turned his head a little and saw Wilcox's body sprawled on the ground beside him and, beyond the body, the pale glow of light and the dark outline of the cabin.

Melissa's hands had stopped, frozen in mid-movement, when he turned his head. She had been crying, sure that he was dead.

"Oh, Mallonee! Darling—"

He brought up one hand unsteadily, trying to touch her hands. "You're—you're all right, Melissa?"

"Oh, yes—yes!" The relief was a sob and a song in her voice. "I grabbed Jeff's gun and I—I followed you."

"You killed Dorsey."

"I had to. He was right on top of you. He was—"

His head was clearing a little. He realized suddenly that she was almost naked, that her face was blue with cold. He could feel the chills go shuddering down her body. He put out an arm to brace himself, rolled, and managed to lift himself to his knees.

"Got to get you inside," he said hoarsely.

The orange light was coming back, wheeling and whirling in dizzying wide circles that swept over him like waves. He saw her come up to her feet, felt her hands beneath his arms, supporting his as he tried to stand. The cabin was very far away, an immense, an immeasurable distance, but they were staggering toward it, her arm strong and sure about him.

"It's a long way," he said huskily. "A long way—"

"We'll make it," she said.

They rounded the corner of the cabin wall and he saw the door standing open to receive them, saw the glow of light, and heat and safety inside. He looked down at her, and smiled.

THE END

www.ingramcontent.com/pod-product-compliance
Lightning Source LLC
Chambersburg PA
CBHW070936250626
47159CB00009B/3267